M000208540

MONTANA SEAL'S
MAIL-ORDER
BRIDE

BROTHERHOOD PROTECTORS

NEW YORK TIMES BESTSELLING AUTHOR
ELLE JAMES

Copyright © 2019 by Elle James

All rights reserved.

No part of this book may be reproduced in any form or by any electronic or mechanical means, including information storage and retrieval systems, without written permission from the author, except for the use of brief quotations in a book review.

Dedicated to my readers who make my dreams come true by keeping me in the business I love dearly...WRITING! I love you all so much. Thank you for buying my books!
Elle James

AUTHOR'S NOTE

Brotherhood Protectors Series

Montana SEAL (#1)

Bride Protector SEAL (#2)

Montana D-Force (#3)

Cowboy D-Force (#4)

Montana Ranger (#5)

Montana Dog Soldier (#6)

Montana SEAL Daddy (#7)

Montana Ranger's Wedding Vow (#8)

Montana SEAL Undercover Daddy (#9)

Cape Cod SEAL Rescue (#10)

Montana SEAL Friendly Fire (#11)

Montana SEAL's Mail-Order Bride (#12)

SEAL Justice (#13)

Ranger Creed (#14)

Delta Force Rescue (#15)

Dog Days of Christmas (#16)

Montana Rescue (#17)

Montana Ranger Returns (#18)

Visit ellejames.com for titles and release dates
and join Elle James's Newsletter

CHAPTER 1

GAVIN STARED out the window of the foreman's office as Hank and Sadie Patterson climbed out of their dark, full-sized SUV. Sadie opened the back door and fiddled inside, finally lifting baby Emma out of her car seat and into her arms.

His chest tightened, and his breathing lodged in his throat. It happened every time he saw Hank, Sadie and Emma together. When he'd been on active duty, he'd thought himself immune to needing a family. Now, approaching thirty-five, single and missing part of one leg, Gavin guessed his chances at what Hank had were slim to none.

"Blackstock!" a female voice sounded behind him.

Gavin started and spun to face Lori Mize, one of the residents at the Brighter Days Rehabilitation Ranch. She leaned heavily on her good leg, her arms crossed over her chest, her bright blue eyes narrowed.

"What's wrong with you? I called your name four times before you turned around. Did one of your *other* disabilities have anything to do with your hearing?"

Anyone without disabilities wouldn't have gotten away with her comment, but Lori knew he was there for the same reasons she'd come to Montana. Transitioning to civilian life after a catastrophic injury such as they'd both received had proven more difficult than they'd imagined. This ranch had better results than most facilities that tried to prepare them for life outside of Uncle Sam's military.

But then Gavin could have never dreamed he'd lose a limb, ending his career as a US Navy SEAL. He turned back to the happy picture Hank, Sadie and Emma made.

Lori crossed to the window and stood beside him. "So stinkin' happy. Almost makes my sweet tooth hurt." She sighed. "But I can't begrudge them their happiness. They deserve it after all they've been through."

"Agreed." Gavin continued to stare at the family. "Ever wonder where you'd be in your life if you hadn't lost your leg?"

Lori's lips pressed into a thin line. "I'd hoped to be married with a kid or two by now." She glanced toward him. "You?"

He shrugged. "What's it matter, anyway? We are who we are."

Her brow furrowing, Lori faced him and cocked her head to one side. "And what is that supposed to mean?"

He nodded toward the Pattersons. "We'll probably never have what they have."

"I don't know what you're talking about. I lost my leg, not my reproductive parts." She patted her belly. "I haven't given up hope on having kids." Her gaze slipped from his and went to Hank.

He shot her a sideways glance. "Interesting. You didn't say anything about marriage."

She lifted one shoulder. "I figure if a man can't accept me for how I am now, I don't need one. I can have a baby without a man," she muttered beneath her breath, but loud enough Gavin caught the words. "Though it would be a lot easier with one."

"Right. I was hellbent on being a lifer as a SEAL. I didn't want to get married and drag a wife around from duty station to duty station while I deployed eleven months out of the year. I didn't think it would be fair."

She glanced at him, one eyebrow arched. "And now that you're not deploying, why don't you date and find you a woman to settle down with?"

"You want to go out with me?" Gavin asked, knowing the answer before she gave it.

"Oh, hell no." Lori shook her head. "It would be like going out with my older brother. Eww." She

studied him. "But there's no reason you can't find someone."

He snorted. "In case you haven't noticed, there aren't that many women around Eagle Rock, Montana. And most of them know I'm missing a leg."

"So?" Lori's brow dipped low on her forehead. "You're saying you don't think a woman can love you because you're one leg short of a pair? Hell, what's that mean for my chances? I'm short one leg, too" She flung her arm in the air. "Guess I'm destined to hit a sperm bank, if I want kids."

"Be serious."

She looked at the Pattersons again and gave a deep sigh. "You want kids?"

He nodded, his gaze going to baby Emma.

The ranch's physical therapist Hannah Kendricks stepped out of the house, smiling at Hank and Sadie. She took Emma in her arms and tickled the baby beneath her chin.

"Sure, I want kids," Gavin said. "But more than that, I want a partner in life. Someone to come home to, to share the ups and downs."

"Someone to love?"

"If I could have it all, yes." Gavin turned away from the scene and paced the office floor. "Maybe I should move to a city where I could meet more women. Women who would be tolerant of my... shortcomings."

Lori gave a bark of laughter. "You? In a city?" She

shook her head. "Not happening. You'd shrivel up and die." Her gaze never left him. "You're serious, aren't you?" She touched his arm. "Gavin, you're a good guy. Your gal just hasn't made her appearance yet."

"And she's not going to. Not out here."

"Shoot, Gavin, how many women have you dated since coming to Montana?"

"None," he said, his tone flat. "There aren't that many out here."

"Maybe you should broaden your horizons. Have you signed up with an online dating site?" Lori asked.

"Hell, no. Have you?" Gavin shot back at her.

"I don't want a mate so badly I'm ready to put myself out there." She shook a finger at him. "Besides, we weren't talking about me. We were talking about your situation. Gavin Blackstock, you're lonely."

"I'm not getting any younger," he said, his jaw hardening. He didn't like admitting that he was lonely. But Lori had hit the nail on the head. "I don't want to put my name on some site, and then meet a woman who has expectations of meeting a whole man. I want to be up front with a woman. She needs to know the truth before we even meet."

"Then do it," Lori urged. "There has to be someone out there for you."

"But I don't want to date. Why can't a guy advertise for a wife, get one and be done with the whole damn thing? Courting is a pain in the ass." He ran a hand through his hair. "Oh, forget about it. It doesn't matter, anyway."

"Gavin, sounds like what you need is a mail-order bride." Lori grinned and plopped down at Gavin's desk and booted up the computer. "I bet there's a place on the internet where you can advertise for a bride. We just have to look."

"No. I'm fine being alone. Sorry I ever opened my mouth."

"The hell you are. Look at you, mooning over Hank and Sadie." Lori clicked on the keys and brought up a browser window. She typed in mail-order bride and waited as suggestions popped up on the screen. "Wow. Who knew there were that many porn sites for mail-order brides? Dang…"

"Just shut it down. I'm not interested. Besides, she'd have to be pretty desperate to agree to be a mail-order bride."

"Wait, here's a site that looks legit." Lori paused and read through the information provided. "All the applicants are vetted to make sure they aren't felons or already married. If they're foreign, they have to have a valid passport. They suggest the parties meet online first, and then arrange a meet and greet in person. If the parties are in agreement, a special license can be obtained, or they can fly to Vegas for a quick wedding." Lori clicked more keys.

"What are you doing?"

"I'm entering your information." She glanced at

him, running her gaze over him from top to toe. "You're what...six-feet tall?"

"Six-one," he corrected. "But stop right now. I'm not interested in marrying a stranger. We might not even be compatible."

"You can enter exactly what you want in a bride. A full list of requirements." She cocked an eyebrow. "So, what's top on your list?"

"Damn it, Lori. I'm not ordering a bride."

She acted as though he hadn't spoken, her lips pursing as she typed. "Must be female with a Y chromosome." She laughed. "You never know."

"Lori..." Gavin gave her his most dangerous tone.

She still wasn't listening. "Must love horses. Must want children. Willing to work hard." She smiled up at Gavin. "Am I right?"

"Yes, but you're missing the point." He clenched his fists. "I'm not marrying a stranger."

Lori glared at him. "You're the one missing the point. If you don't put yourself out there, you won't get anything." She raised her cell phone and snapped a picture of him. Then she typed more information onto the screen and hit enter.

Gavin stared over her shoulder. "What did you just do?" A screen popped up congratulating Gavin Blackstock on joining the site. "You didn't."

Lori pushed away from the desk and out of range of Gavin's hands. "Now, you wait and see if you get a live one. I'll be back later to go through the responses with you."

He scowled. "I'll reject every one of them. You're wasting my time and theirs."

"At least, give it a week and see what comes of it."

"I'm not giving it anything. I'm not ordering my bride through the internet like a goddamn bag of dogfood."

Lori patted his cheek. "Just you wait. I have a feeling about this. I think you're going to get lucky and find the right woman for you." She smiled. "Then you can thank me." She winked and darted up from the chair before Gavin could grab her and strangle the life out of her.

What the hell had Lori gotten him into? He leaned over the computer and read the ad.

Wanted: Bride to live on a ranch in Montana. Must be willing to work hard and bear children. Undaunted groom, one leg short of a pair, loyal and respectful.

"Great. I sound like a pathetic, desperate loser."

Lori laughed. "I was thinking you sounded more like a Labrador retriever." She patted him on the arm. "I bet you get a number of hits before the end of the week."

"Whoever answers that ad has to be another pathetic and desperate loser." Gavin shook his head. "I'm not going through with this."

"Give it a chance," Lori said. "At least, see who

responds. Who knows? You might find the woman of your dreams."

Gavin snorted. "More like my nightmares."

OLIVIA AURELIA ST. George sat in the church after everyone else had gone except her best friend Lilianna and her bodyguard Collin. She stared down at her hands with the white handkerchief crumpled in her grip and studied the contrast between it and her black dress. Guilt stabbed her in the heart. They had been good men. She hadn't loved them, but that hadn't been a requirement. They had been willing to marry her. "This is all my fault."

Lilianna covered her hands with one of her own. "You can't say that. You didn't drive the car that killed Andrew. Someone else did."

"If he hadn't agreed to marry me, he wouldn't have been where he was when that car hit him."

"Again, it's not your fault. They'll catch the driver," Lilianna said. "Just wait." Her words were hopeful, but the tone wasn't.

Olivia shook her head. "When? They never found the man who pushed Ian into the path of an oncoming bus." She looked up into Lilianna's eyes. "Two fiancés, two deaths. This is not a coincidence. The law states that if I don't find a husband and start producing heirs by my 30th birthday, the throne goes to the next in line. It's hopeless."

"You'll find a husband. And you still have time to get pregnant," Lilianna took her hands in hers. "Don't give up now. You have ten months to make it all happen."

Ten months. To get married and have a child. Ten months. It would take a miracle to find a man who would agree to marry her when both fiancés she'd had were now dead. What man in his right mind would sign up for that?

"Why don't you look at one of those online dating sites?" Lilianna suggested. She pulled out her cell phone and searched online dating.

"I don't really have much time to date. One month to marry and get started making a baby isn't going to work. I might as well give up."

"No way." Lilianna stared across at her. "You can't let your cousin Rupert take the throne. He's not fit to be a ruler."

"And I am? I can't even find a man to marry and propagate the line." Olivia sighed. "I hate the thought that this would disappoint my father. I know how much he would have wanted me to be the next queen of Lastovia, given the circumstances of my brother's demise."

"Darling, he groomed you since you were born."

Olivia closed her eyes for a moment. "He groomed my brother. Besides, we're only figureheads anymore these days. I wish it still wasn't so important who rules."

"Because people looked up to your father, your brother and now, you. In such trying times, they like to have a monarch who understands their needs and represents them in the world."

"Sometimes, I wish I was just a regular person. Then I'd fall in love and live happily ever after."

Lilianna snorted. "There's no guarantee on the happily-ever-after, even for us mere mortals." Lilianna frowned and keyed into her phone. "Okay... so you don't have time to do the dating roulette game. How about one of those mail-order bride sites? You can skip the dating and get right down to the marriage and children part."

"The only men who sign up for those sites are desperate."

"Exactly," Lilianna said. "No questions asked, just get married and make a baby."

Olivia shook her head. "I can't do this."

"Just humor me, will you?" Lilianna said. "Here you go. Bachelor number one lives in England. He's a professor of history and likes playing cribbage. Sounds boring, but manageable." She scrolled down through the man's details.

Olivia grabbed the phone from her and looked at the man's picture. "No way. He has to be sixty years old. And look, he doesn't want children."

Lilianna took the phone back from Olivia.

"Scratch bachelor number one. Oh, look. Bachelor number two is from Louisiana in the US. He's twice divorced, has two teenaged sons and is looking for a woman who likes hunting and race car driving." She looked up. "He has two sons. That means he's fertile. He's not horrible to look at, and he's a mechanic, so he's bound to be good at fixing things."

"I'm not into hunting, and speed makes me nervous." She shook her head. "Besides, he probably doesn't want to start over with an infant if he already has teenaged sons. Give it up, Lilianna."

"I refuse to have your cousin as my king." She kept looking at the phone. "Wait, I've got the man for you. He's never been married."

"No woman would have him…?"

"He's good-looking," Lilianna went on.

"Then he's probably a man who always has to be in control. Maybe even abusive."

"He's from the US, the state of Montana." Lilianna switched apps on her phone. "Where is Montana?"

"A state in the northwest. Known for its cold weather and miles and miles of nothing. There's not much out there, until you get to the western side of the state where all the mountains are. Even then, not many people live in Montana, from what I recall of my geography class."

"Wouldn't that be perfect?" Lilianna's face lit in a grin. "Sounds like it's way out in the middle of nowhere. A place you could get lost in. Whoever is sabotaging you won't find you there." She practically jumped up and down on her seat. "It's just what you need."

"I'm not going to Montana. I'm not marrying a stranger," Olivia said.

Lilianna switched back to the mail-order bride app and held up her hand. "Listen to this. If this isn't perfect, I don't know what is." She wiped the smile off her face and read out loud.

Wanted: Bride to live on a ranch in Montana. Must be willing to work hard and bear children.

"He sounds like a cowboy from way back in the old American west of the 1800s."

An image of a man wearing a cowboy hat and chaps rose in Olivia's mind. She wouldn't admit that she was intrigued. She'd spent many an evening watching old westerns on her television and had dreamed like many young girls of being rescued by a man on a white horse and riding off into the sunset.

"Look at him," Lilianna said. "He's even good looking. That strong chin and piercing eyes." She sighed. "If you don't go after him, I just might."

Olivia took the phone from her and glanced down at the image, hating to admit Lilianna was right. The man looked at her as if staring into her very soul. Awareness rippled through her body, coiling tightly in her belly.

"Caught your interest, didn't he," Lilianna whispered.

He had.

Olivia read the ad again.

Wanted: Bride to live on a ranch in Montana. Must be willing to work hard and bear children.

She scrolled further down to the part Lilianna hadn't read aloud.

Undaunted groom, one leg short of a pair, loyal and respectful.

She frowned, squinted and read it again. "You didn't read this part."

Lilianna leaned over her shoulder. "I didn't see it."

"What do you think this means—one leg short of a pair?"

"One leg short..." Lilianna's eyes rounded. "He only has one leg." Her face fell. "Well, shoot. And I thought we had a winner."

Olivia read more of the man's background. "Prior military, Purple Heart recipient. Lili, he lost his leg serving his country."

"Sounds like an honorable man. But we can keep looking." She reached for the cell phone.

Olivia turned away without giving it back. Something about the former warrior's face resonated with something deep inside herself. "No. I don't want to look at another."

"Fine. Then we go through a list of all of your acquaintances. Surely, there's a man amongst them who would make a suitable partner and father."

"No," Olivia said. "Actually, I think everything

you've been saying is right. I need to find a place where I can remain out of the public's eye."

"If you mean hide, then you're right." Lilianna paced the church aisle. "Where would be the best place to hide for the next ten months? Preferably a place with eligible bachelors. Eligible, desperate bachelors."

An idea took root and blossomed in Olivia's chest. She sat in one of the pews, hunkered over the phone and began typing.

"Olivia?"

"Shh." She kept typing, concentrating on what she wanted to say. Then she held up the phone, snapped a picture of herself and submitted her response.

"Olivia?" Lilianna snatched the phone from her hands. "What have you done?"

"I think I just accepted a proposal of marriage." Her heart pounded against her ribs, and she felt just a little queasy. But not nearly as nauseated as she'd felt every time she'd said yes to her two previous fiancés. What she'd just done was perhaps the most spontaneous and...crazy thing she'd ever done in her life. But sometimes, a person had to step outside the lines in order to make things happen.

"Sweetie, what have you done?"

"You can read my response. It's out there, but I didn't use my full name. I used the name Aurelia George."

Lilianna found her response and fell into a pew, her face pale.

"Woman with biological clock ticking seeks groom with a family in mind. Willing to work hard and bear children. When can we meet?"

"Oh, dear Lord. You're kidding, right?" Lilianna shook her head and the stared at Olivia. "Please tell me this is all a bad dream."

Olivia's lips twisted. "Lili, this was your idea. Don't tell me you're having second thoughts."

"But he's only got one leg," she whispered.

"Therefore, he's got to be a little desperate. I need a man who's just desperate enough to make this work." Olivia smiled, feeling more lighthearted than she had in months. She waved to the man standing guard at the door to the little church. "Collin," she called out.

The man checked out the window beside the exit before he turned to join Olivia in the aisles. "Yes, ma'am."

"Are you up for a visit to the US?" She slid a side-eye in his direction. Olivia had done a thorough background check on Collin O'Bannon, but she couldn't remember everything. Only that he'd come highly recommended as a bodyguard. "You're from somewhere in the US, correct?"

"Yes. Maine."

"Good." She leaned close. "Ever been to Montana?"

He nodded. "Went elk hunting there with my father."

Hunting was a good, outdoor sport. But she needed him to be closer than a neighbor, if she was going to pull this off. "Ever done any ranching?"

"As a matter of fact…no."

"Do you know anything about horses or cattle?"

"Only that one we eat, and the other we don't."

She chewed on her bottom lip.

"You're not seriously considering marrying this one-legged cowboy from Montana, are you?"

A hope bloomed in Olivia's chest and spread outward until it lit her face with a smile. "That's exactly what I'm considering." She grabbed Lilianna's hand. "Come on, we have a lot to do in a short amount of time, if Mr. Gavin Blackstock accepts my response."

CHAPTER 2

Two days later...

Gavin paced the length of the sidewalk in front of the bus station, forcing himself to walk with as little of a limp as possible. He'd been walking with a prosthetic leg for over two years, long enough he should have mastered it by now. Hell, it didn't matter. He'd laid it on the line in his advertisement. Or rather, Lori had. *One leg short of a pair.* Holy shit. He couldn't believe he'd actually received a response to that nonsense. "I can't believe I let you talk me into this. It's the stupidest thing I've done in my entire life."

"Give the woman a chance." Lori stood nearby, her gaze on the main road leading into Eagle Rock, Montana. "You saw her photo. She's not bad looking. In fact, she's beautiful."

"In that case, what's wrong with her?" Gavin couldn't believe the first day his advertisement had been posted that he'd received over fifty proposals. He'd reviewed each one out of morbid curiosity, with no intention of taking any one of the women as his wife. Just how many desperate women were out there? He suspected as many as there were desperate men. Including him.

By the time he'd found Aurelia's photo and response, all of the women had turned into a hazy blur of faces. "This is ludicrous," he'd said. "You can't advertise for a wife. It has to be done the old-fashioned way through dating and getting to know each other."

Lori rolled her eyes. "In that case, you'll die alone. Move." She'd taken his seat at the desk in the foreman's office. "When is Percy getting back from vacation?"

"Tomorrow. And I imagine he won't appreciate that you and I have commandeered his office and computer for other than ranch business."

"He'll get over it. It's all for a good cause." Lori bent to the task of wading through all the applicants for the position of Mrs. Gavin Blackstock.

Gavin had been on the verge of laughing, but the joke was too much on him to be funny.

"What do you think about this one?" Lori pointed at the screen.

Gavin shook his head. "I could never marry a

woman with a nose ring. It reminds me too much of the rings they used to put in bulls' noses. I would never be able to look at her without that image popping into my mind. Not that I have anything against her piercings or tattoos." He held up his hands. "But no. I couldn't marry her."

"She might be a really nice woman."

"Sorry."

"How about her?" Lori brought up the next contestant. "She's your age, likes the outdoors and wants children."

"No blue hair."

"Hair color can change," Lori muttered. "Okay, okay, moving on." After Lori had clicked through half a dozen other responses, she paused, her brow dipping. "Hold the press," she said, her tone laced with excitement. "I think we have a winner."

"We don't have a winner. I'm not going through with this. I can't marry a complete stranger."

"Listen to this," Lori continued.

Woman with biological clock ticking seeks groom with a family in mind. Willing to work hard and bear children. When can we meet?

"So? Sounds like all the rest."

"But she's not like all the rest." Lori looked up, a grin filling her face. "She looks positively normal. Well, a little better than normal. She's beautiful."

Intrigued, Gavin leaned over Lori's shoulder, his curiosity getting the better of him.

Lori was right. The woman had long, wavy blond hair, and the most incredibly blue eyes that stared back at him from the computer screen.

He'd felt as if she were looking straight into his soul and knew everything there was to know about him.

Deep inside, though he'd never admit it, the woman's image had touched Gavin.

Still, he couldn't believe they had taken it this far. Within a week of submitting the advertisement, he was about to meet his mail-order bride.

"You tell any of the guys back at Brighter Days that she's a mail-order bride, and I'll personally make your life a living hell."

"I told you, your secret is safe with me," Lori chuckled. "Look at you. The unflappable Gavin Blackstock is shaking more than a baby rattlesnake with a new button."

"I'm not shaking," he grumbled and ran his hand through his hair for the fifth time since they'd arrived at the bus station. "This is a mistake. I can't believe I let you talk me into this."

"What's the worst that could happen?" Lori asked.

"She could have posted someone else's picture," Gavin stated, his tone flat, his brows descending.

"If she did, no worries. You gave each other the option to back out if you meet and you change your minds."

"What if I can't stand her, but she still wants to go through with this farce?"

"Then you have the option to back out." Lori gripped his arms and stared into his eyes. "Hey, big guy, it's going to be all right. Just give her a chance." Lori's eyes lit. "Oh, look. There's the bus now." She hooked Gavin's arm, turning him toward the approaching vehicle of doom.

Gavin backed away a step.

Lori held tightly to his arm, her smile stiffening. "You're not running away. She's come a long way, the least you can do is meet the woman."

"She probably has a rap sheet longer than my arm."

"The mail-order bride site vets their applicants. They did a thorough background check on the woman."

"She could have fed them lies. False name, false address. She could have stolen a dead person's ID."

"Again, you don't have to go through with anything, but it won't hurt to meet the woman." Lori locked her arm around his. "And the bonus is that our new ranch hand is arriving on the same bus. Bet you didn't remember that."

"Ranch hand?" Gavin's eyes narrowed. "What ranch hand?"

"You don't remember Percy advertising for a ranch hand now that the senator is backing Brighter Days? Management thinks they'll need more help."

"I thought the idea behind the ranch was to let the recovering veterans do the work."

Lori nodded. "It's still the concept. But you have to admit that when Percy is gone, some of the more difficult work piles up."

"I'm there," Gavin argued. "I help. I don't know why he thinks we need another full-time ranch hand."

"From what I understand, Collin Banner needs this job as much as we need him."

"Ahh. A paid guest?"

Lori shrugged. "From what I read in his letter to Hannah."

"So, now you're reading Hannah's mail?" Gavin stared at the woman he thought he knew.

Again, Lori shrugged. "I might have been in her office when she was reading it. And I might have looked over her shoulder when I put the next day's mail on her desk."

The bus rolled to a stop in front of the small bus station. Martin Sims, the man who sold bus tickets at the bus station and also ran the local newspaper, stepped out of his office and pushed his Colorado Rockies baseball cap to the back of his head and stretched. "Only ten minutes late. I'd say that makes for a good day."

As the bus door opened, Gavin's gut twisted into a solid knot, and he held his breath, fully expecting his worst nightmare to step down.

A woman who had to be in her fifties, carrying an oversized tote bag filled with yarn and knitting needles was first to step down onto the sidewalk.

Gavin stiffened.

"Seriously, dude," Lori hissed. "Get a grip. It's not her."

A man about Gavin's age, with broad shoulders, muscular arms and thighs was next out. He carried a camouflage backpack and wore sunglasses. He glanced around, his face turning toward Gavin and Lori.

Because his eyes were hidden by the mirror shades, Gavin couldn't get a reading on him. But he appeared to be prior-military by the way he carried himself—shoulders back, chin up, fists clenched in a loose ball. And the camouflage backpack had to be a carryover from his active duty days.

The man headed toward Gavin. "You wouldn't happen to be from the Brighter Days Ranch, would you?"

Gavin nodded, only half-listening to the man, because his attention was still focused on the bus door.

Lori held out her hand. "We are. I'm Lori Mize, one of the long-term guests. You must be Collin Banner."

Collin gripped her hand in a firm shake. "I am. I'm your new ranch hand." He released Lori's hand and held out his hand to Gavin.

"Gavin Blackstock, assistant foreman," Gavin said, taking his focus off the bus long enough to shake hands with Banner. When he turned his attention back, he was disappointed to see the bus driver climbing down to shake hands with Martin Sims.

That was it?

His brow furrowing, Gavin exchanged a glance with Lori.

She shrugged.

"I have to collect my duffel bag, and then I'll be ready to go," Banner said.

The bus driver opened the undercarriage of the bus and pulled out a tattered, plaid suitcase and set it down in front of the woman with the bag of yarn. Then he reached into the bus again and pulled out a drab green duffel bag.

Banner grabbed the bag and slipped it over his shoulder. "That's it for me."

What the hell? Gavin glanced at the bus door again. Had he been stood up by his bride? Relief, disappointment and a spike of anger warred inside him. When he should be happy the woman was a no-show, he was disappointed he'd been proven right. You couldn't order a bride over the internet. It just didn't happen that way.

He shot another glance toward the woman with the yarn when she stood there, without moving. Surely, she wasn't his bride. Just to be certain, he said the name loud enough she could hear and respond if it truly was her. "Aurelia."

The woman tilted her head to the side. "Pardon me? Did you say something?"

"Aurelia?" he asked.

The older woman's face lit in a smile. "Oh, that's rich." She slapped a hand to her thigh and laughed. "You think I'm Aurelia?"

Heat flowed up Gavin's neck into his cheeks. "No, ma'am. My apologies."

"I'm not Aurelia." The older woman tipped her head toward the bus door. "But she is."

Gavin turned in time to see a pair of long, shapely legs lead their owner down the steps of the bus to the sidewalk. The woman wore a tan trench coat. The hem of a powder-blue dress hung down below the coat and blue shoes matched the dress perfectly. A soft cream-colored scarf covered her head and shoulders, hiding her face from sight.

Then she pushed the scarf off her head and shook her long blond hair free. When she turned to face Gavin, he forgot how to breathe.

Aurelia George was everything and more than the photo she'd posted on the mail-order bride website.

Suddenly, Gavin couldn't think, couldn't move, couldn't come up with words to greet his prospective bride. Then it hit him like a steamroller.

This knockout was his prospective bride. Holy hell! Now, what was he supposed to do?

"Bingo," Lori said softly, and then leaned close. "Close your mouth, Gavin," she whispered. "You look like a halfwit."

CHAPTER 3

Olivia Aurelia St. George blinked against the bright Montana sunshine and smiled. The air was clean, the sky was bluer than any sky she could ever remember seeing, and she'd made it to Montana without being followed. So far, her plan was working. Now, all she had to do was convince her groom she was the real deal, and that she wanted to marry posthaste and start on that family.

When the bus had pulled to a stop, she'd been so excited about finally arriving that she'd knocked her purse over and spilled the entire contents all over the floor. It had taken her several minutes to find her belongings. Stepping down from the bus, she'd been shocked to see the man she was hanging all her hopes on was much better looking than his photograph. Not in a GQ way, but in a wickedly rugged way that set her heart pounding and her pulse on fire.

Now that she was in Montana and facing the man she was to marry, what did she do next?

She shot a glance at Collin, thankful he'd worked with the owner-manager of the Brighter Days Rehabilitation Ranch to secure a job there as a recovering veteran. It wasn't a far stretch from the truth. Collin still had nightmares and flashbacks from his deployments.

Having Collin there, allayed her initial fear that she would land in Montana and not know a soul and be completely exposed to any danger that might arise.

Collin had fixed that with an email and a phone call to Hannah Kendricks. And he'd done a background check on the physical therapist, learning that her father was a senator for the state of Montana. He'd also run a background check on Gavin Blackstock, her groom. Working with some contacts he had in the military, he found that Gavin was a decorated veteran Navy SEAL who'd lost his leg on a dangerous mission in Afghanistan. A mission in which he'd sacrificed his own safety to insure his teammates got out alive. The details weren't readily available because the mission had been classified Top Secret. But his contacts got the scuttlebutt on the basics.

What it came down to was Gavin Blackstock was the real deal. He was what he'd put in his advertisement...and so much more.

Olivia had assumed her second name and dropped St. off St. George. Collin had also arranged to have a passport made with her assumed name Aurelia George from Bar Harbor, Maine. They'd dreamed up a background to explain why her accent clearly wasn't northeastern, but more British English. Her mother was from London and met her father when he was in the Air Force on active duty, stationed at Mildenhall in the United Kingdom.

Oliva...no, she had to start thinking of herself as Aurelia...which wasn't too hard, considering her father had always preferred calling her Aurelia. After Lilianna had gotten over the shock of Aurelia's commitment to her plan, she and Collin had come up with her cover story, her background and her plan for sneaking out of the country, undetected.

The undetected part had been a challenge. Thankfully, she and Lilianna were the same height. They'd gone into a ladies' restroom in a shopping mall, switched clothing and headscarves and left at different times. Lilianna had gone out first, left the mall and climbed into the waiting limousine Aurelia usually traveled in. Collin had gone with her, despite his better judgment. Aurelia had slipped out of the back of the mall, got into a taxi and headed for the train station with her fake passport.

Collin had someone preposition her suitcase at the train station. Once he had Lilianna back at the royal palace and tucked away in Aurelia's suite of rooms, Collin had left the palace, gone to a local pub and slipped out the back. He'd changed into different clothes, wore a baseball cap low over his face and joined Aurelia at the train station. Together, but separately, they boarded a highspeed train to Frankfurt, Germany, sitting in different seats in the same car.

Aurelia wore a scarf over her hair and half her face and pretended to sleep, though she was wide awake and aware of every person getting on and off the train.

By the time they reached Frankfurt, she was already exhausted from nerves. They'd planned to be on the plane to the US within two hours of arriving at the airport.

Careful to keep her face covered, she wore fake glasses and the scarf everywhere she went, not wanting cameras to pick up on her whereabouts. Maybe she was being overly careful, but two of her suitors had died trying to marry her. She didn't want a third fiancé to be the next target, nor did she want whoever was sabotaging her plans to come after her. She had an obligation to her country, and by God, she'd fulfill that obligation, even if it meant marrying a man she didn't know and hiding for the next nine or ten months in the wilds of Montana to have a baby.

Hell, she hadn't thought about it, but where did women have their babies out here? Did they hire midwives to deliver? She knew there was a well-equipped hospital in Bozeman, but would she be able to get from the ranch to Bozeman once her contractions were underway? If she got pregnant in the next month, that would put her having her baby near the end of spring. Would her baby be born in a late-spring blizzard? She'd researched Montana. The state was known for unpredictable weather. They had snow as late as July.

But as she stepped out of the bus, all her worries were pushed to the back of her mind. Her future husband stood beside Collin and a pretty woman with light red hair and blue eyes. Granted, the woman wore jeans and a plaid shirt, and her hair was pulled back in a loose ponytail. But her smile lit her face, making her quite attractive.

Who was she to Gavin Blackstock? Considering he'd advertised for a wife, she wasn't in the running for the job, nor was she wearing a ring. And she appeared pleased to see Aurelia. All of this rushed through her head, almost wiping away her and Gavin's plan to pretend they've known each other for a long time. Now was the time for her to put on a show. She and Gavin had discussed the strategy online before she'd agreed to come. As a royal, she was used to playing a part in public. But this part was far more personal than any she'd been tasked to perform in the past. Squaring her shoulders, she pasted a huge smile on her face and flung her arms around Gavin's neck. "Gavin, darling, I'm so glad to see you. I could barely wait to get here."

Gavin settled his hands on her waist and replied, "It's good to see you too, A-aurelia."

A bubble of laughter rose up Aurelia's chest, and she let it go. The man was obviously embarrassed and maybe a little shy, which she found endearing.

A spark of something rippled from where their bodies touched and spread heat to the very tips of her extremities. Aurelia sucked in a breath and held it, afraid to let it go lest she gasp.

Gavin was as solid as a rock and made her feel surprisingly protected. His grip was firm but gentle for such a big guy, and he didn't release her immediately. He leaned back a little and stared for a long moment into her eyes, as if searching for something. Just like when she'd looked into those eyes in the picture on the internet, she could feel the same connection, as if he was looking into her soul.

She released the breath she'd held.

"Aurelia, we've waited far too long," Gavin said, his tone low, resonant and as rich and thick as melted chocolate, seeping into every pore of her skin.

Awareness made her shiver. Aurelia hadn't expected such a swift and visceral reaction to this stranger. And frankly, it frightened her at the same time as it excited her.

In their correspondence over the internet, they'd agreed to keep their arrangement between themselves until they'd had a chance to meet and determine whether a match could be made. They would both have the opportunity to back out, should they decide their proposal wouldn't work.

So far, Aurelia was still agreeable to the marriage, and even more convinced he was exactly what she needed. She wondered if Gavin would take a little more convincing.

Finally, he released her and stepped back, keeping a hand at the small of her back.

The woman beside him, held out her hand. "Hello, I'm Lori Mize, one of the guests at the Brighter Days Rehab Ranch. Don't mind me," she said with a smile. "I came along to meet you. Gavin kept talking about this wonderful girlfriend of his. We all thought she didn't exist." Lori winked. "I'm happy to see you really do." Lori shook her hand with a strong grip and a lot of enthusiasm. "And you're very pretty. Who would have thought Gavin would have a pretty girlfriend stashed away somewhere?"

"Nice to meet you, Ms. Mize," Aurelia said.

"You can call me Lori. We're not too formal around here." Lori turned to Collin. "And this is our brand new ranch hand, Collin Banner. You two might have met on the bus?" Lori cocked an eyebrow.

"No, I'm sorry, we haven't met." Heat threatened to rise up Aurelia's neck. She focused on not feeling guilty for lying about knowing Collin. She held out her hand. "Nice to meet you."

Collin shook her hand, giving it an extra, reassuring squeeze. "Pleasure, ma'am."

Gavin waved a hand toward a large, black king cab pickup. "If you two are ready, we can head on out to the ranch."

"I just have to get my luggage," Aurelia said and turned to the three new, matching cases the bus driver had set out on the curb. She'd had to leave most of her clothes and toiletries at home in Lastovia. In order to sneak out of the country, she'd had to leave with what she wore, the suitcase Collin had pre-positioned at the train station and the fake passport, praying she wasn't caught and thrown in jail along the way for falsifying legal documents.

Their first stop in the US had been in New York City where she'd had to buy enough clothing and toiletries to last her for the year she'd be in Montana. Unsure of what the wild western state had to offer, she'd stocked up on everything she thought she might need, including several pairs of blue jeans, boots and a heavy winter coat. Though it was late summer, she'd heard the winters could be long and brutal. Her own country was quite cool in the winter, so she wasn't worried about how to deal with the cold.

She was worried about taking too long to get to the part where they promised to marry and start making babies. Though she'd arrive in the country under a forged passport, she would make certain she signed her marriage certificate with her full, legal name. Otherwise, all her efforts to marry and produce an heir by her birthday deadline would be null and void.

Lori took one look at the three suitcases and laughed. "I guess you've come to stay."

Aurelia's gaze captured Gavin's. "That was the plan," she said softly, daring him to say otherwise. He could back out, though she prayed he wouldn't.

If she had a lot of time to court the man, she would. And she'd tell him why she needed to marry and get started on having babies, but that might make him even more inclined to back out of the deal. The man would probably be uncomfortable being a part of a royal family. And who said they couldn't be married and live separately? The law of her country didn't say the spouse had to live in Lastovia. Just that the royal had to be married and produce an heir by his or her thirtieth birthday. For that matter, would Gavin want to live that far away from his children?

Gavin gathered two of the suitcases in his hands. When he tried to juggle the third, Collin snatched it out of his reach and carried it to the pickup.

Aurelia and Lori followed the men.

"Just so you know," Lori whispered, "I'm the only other person on the ranch who knows your secret."

Aurelia shot a wide-eyed glance at the woman who limped along beside her. Her secret? Did she know she was a royal and that she was there to

fulfill her family obligation in order to inherit her throne? "And how do you feel about it?" she asked vaguely, not offering any more details about anything.

"I think the idea of a mail-order bride is exactly what Gavin needed. Otherwise, he would have given up completely on the idea of marriage and a family. He has some dumb idea that a woman wouldn't find him husband material because he's missing one measly leg."

Aurelia studied Gavin's back and legs as he carried the two heavy suitcases. "He seems to get along just fine without it. Why should that bother me?"

Lori shrugged, limping along beside Aurelia. "You never know how people will react to people who are different from them."

Aurelia's focus shifted from Gavin to Lori, and she frowned. "You speak as if from experience."

Lori bent and tapped her knuckles against the lower half of her left leg, making a sound like knocking against metal.

Aurelia's eyes widened. "You, too?"

Lori nodded. "My supply truck rolled over an IED. I was the lucky one."

"Losing a leg isn't what I consider lucky," Aurelia said.

"I lost my leg..." Lori looked away. "My battle buddy lost his life."

Aurelia touched her arm. "I'm sorry. I can't even begin to imagine how you feel."

Lori shrugged. "Like it should have been me. I should have been the one to die. Landers had a wife and kid back home. I had no one depending on me. If I hadn't insisted on driving the last leg of the journey, he'd be alive today."

"And you wouldn't be." Aurelia sighed.

"I tell myself there has to be a reason I was spared, and he wasn't. I just haven't found that reason yet." She nodded toward Gavin. "We just have to learn to live a different life than what we had planned." Lori gave Aurelia a tight smile. "Gavin and I have it easy. We have a guy at Brighter Days who's lost a lot more."

Aurelia had thought a lot about Gavin's profile, *One leg short of a pair.* She knew it wouldn't bother her that he was missing a limb. But she hadn't thought about what the loss of a limb had cost the man. Based on what Lori was saying, it was a lot more than the physical aspect.

When they arrived at the truck, the men tossed the suitcases in the bed. Gavin opened the passenger door and held out a hand to help Aurelia up into the seat. Collin held the back door open for Lori and waited until she climbed in before walking around to the opposite side and climbing into the backseat beside her.

Aurelia settled into her seat and waited for Gavin

to slip into the driver's seat. She had a lot to learn about her future husband, assuming he intended to follow through with their wedding plans. If all went smoothly, they would spend a couple days getting acquainted before they made the decision. Then they'd go from there to plan a wedding.

Aurelia couldn't believe how smoothly escaping Lastovia and traveling all the way to Montana had gone. Almost too smoothly. She kept looking for the hitch in her plan. But so far, none had surfaced. Still, she would not let down her guard for a moment. Collin had promised to keep an eye on her, but just as importantly, he'd help protect Gavin from any threat that might arise once they announced their engagement.

CHAPTER 4

GAVIN COULDN'T BELIEVE the woman sitting in the truck beside him was serious. She was absolutely gorgeous. Why did she need to resort to a mail-order method of finding a man to marry? What was the catch? There had to be one. She could have any man her heart desired. Why him...a one-legged former Navy SEAL?

As soon as he had a chance, he'd pull her aside and ask all the questions. Unfortunately, once they were at the ranch, they'd be hard pressed to find a quiet moment alone. Perhaps his first test of his prospective bride would be to find out if she could ride a horse. He'd take her riding and get that alone-time they so desperately needed to get to know one another. Lori had helped him come up with a time-line. A week had seemed reasonable to determine whether they were compatible. After that week, they could decide if they would continue to take their relationship to the next level.

Hell, Gavin didn't think the woman would make it the week. She'd figure out pretty quickly that *he* didn't belong in *her* life and she didn't belong in *his*. He sighed, shifted into drive and headed out to the Brighter Days Rehab Ranch.

All the way to the ranch, he couldn't think of a darned thing to say. Not one thing. And he was supposed to know Aurelia. If he couldn't think of something now, what would happen when the rest of the crew at Brighter Days converged on them? They'd know immediately he had just met Aurelia. Then how would it look if they did end up tying the knot? Not that he cared. He wanted what so many other guys had...a wife and family.

Oh, who was he kidding? This wasn't the way to do it. Lori was wrong.

Lori leaned over the back seat and smiled at Aurelia. "I'm curious, how did you two meet?"

Gavin wanted to reach back and strangle Lori. In the rearview mirror, he could see Lori's lopsided grin. She was testing them with questions the others would shoot at him as soon as they arrived at the ranch. If they didn't have their story straight, now, they never would. What was it they'd agreed on as a cover story?

"We met when our families vacationed on the California coast one year," Aurelia said. She gave Gavin a tight smile.

He nodded, picking up where she left off. "We kept in touch all these years."

"So, are you from California?" Lori asked.

Aurelia glanced out the window. "No, we were only visiting that year."

"Where are you from?" Lori asked, pointblank.

"My parents were diplomats," Aurelia said. "We spent much of my life in Europe."

"That's interesting," Lori said with a smile. "Where are your parents now?"

For a moment Aurelia didn't respond. Instead, she looked ahead at the road in front of them. Then she drew in a deep breath and let it go. "They died two years ago when their car ran off a cliff."

The deadpan way Aurelia spoke of the death of her parents made Gavin shoot a glance her way. She still stared at the road ahead, but her eyes were shadowed, and her lovely smile had disappeared.

Gavin found himself wishing Lori hadn't asked the question that made the sunshine leave Aurelia's face. He frowned at Lori in the rearview mirror.

Lori shrugged.

Beside him Aurelia smiled again, albeit it looked a little forced. "What about you, Gavin? How are your parents. It's been so long since."

"They passed several years ago. Mom had canc

Aurelia reached out a hand and touched his arn "I'm so sorry. She was such a wonderful woman."

Gavin nodded. Hating that they were acting a lie. But his mother had been a good person. "My father died shortly after of a broken heart." They hadn't lived to see their son blown apart. Gavin was just as glad they hadn't had to live through that, though he could have used a friend when he'd been told the doctors had to amputate.

For the longest time, he was convinced he'd have been better off dead, and had even considered ending it. No one would have missed him. He was an only child, with no family left to mourn his death, no wife or children waiting for him to come home.

His physical therapist at Walter Reed had suggested he check into Brighter Days Rehab Ranch. He'd been resistant at first, but the therapist knew Hannah and her ability to work with wounded warriors. Because he'd wanted to get back out west where he'd grown up, Gavin had agreed to give the ranch a shot.

Within days of working with Hannah, Percy and the rescue horses, he'd begun to realize he had more to give to the world now than when he'd still possessed both legs. He had a new appreciation for everything. Hannah had helped him to understand how fortunate he was to have one good leg. One of

the other guests on the ranch was missing both legs. Though Gavin had sustained catastrophic injuries, his spine had remained intact, and he wasn't paralyzed. So what if he had to strap on a prosthetic device that allowed him to walk upright? He could be a lot worse off.

He had a lot more questions for Aurelia, but they would have to wait until she'd run the gauntlet of Hannah and the others at the ranch. Gavin hoped and prayed their flimsy story held up under Hannah's scrutiny. She was one very smart woman, used to dealing with men who faked physical and internal pain.

"What about you, Collin?" Lori switched her interrogation from Aurelia to the new ranch hand. "I understand you did time in the military like most of us at Brighter Days. What branch? How many years? And did you get out on your own, or was decision made for you?"

Collin laughed. "Are you always so..."

"Nosey?" Gavin offered.

"I was going to say curious," Collin said with a smile. "I was in the Army."

"Really?" Lori grinned. "Me, too. What was your MOS?"

"I was 18 Bravo. Eight years active duty. Got out on my own, after five rotations to the Middle East."

Lori's brows rose. "Special Forces. I'm impressed. Ever do any missions with the Navy SEALs?" She

tipped her head toward Gavin. "Gavin, here, was a SEAL."

Collin nodded. "I did one joint mission with a group of SEALs. But I can't talk about it."

"If you tell me, you'd have to kill me, right?" Lori grinned.

Gavin wished he had the ability to be as open and direct as Lori. She could talk to a rock and get a response. Instead, he sat behind the steering wheel, pretending it took all his concentration to maneuver the curves out to the ranch. He shot a glance toward his intended bride. She was staring out at the scenery ahead.

"Is it always this beautiful in Montana?" Aurelia chose that moment to turn toward Gavin, a smile filling her face and what appeared to be a sense of wonder. The Crazy Mountains of Montana had that effect on many who came to see them for the first time.

"It's not quite this peaceful in the wintertime, especially when it's snowing sideways, and you can't see your hand in front of your face," Gavin said. "But we still have to tend to the animals. They can't take care of themselves."

Aurelia nodded. "What kind of animals do you have at the ranch?"

"The usual. Cattle, horses, chickens and a couple of hogs," Gavin said.

"And a couple of dogs and barn cats," Lori added.

"Lori is our dog whisperer," Gavin said.

"I love dogs. I had one growing up," Aurelia's smile turned a little sad.

"Just one?" Lori laughed. "My mother finally had to say no to the strays I brought home when we were up to six dogs in the house."

"We were always so busy, someone else usually had to take care of the dog." Aurelia rubbed her hands on her arms. "I always felt welcomed when I got home. Mikki was always happy to see me." She cast a shy smile over her shoulder. "I didn't realize how much I missed her, until now."

"That's what I love about dogs," Lori said. "They don't care if your hair is combed or you're wearing makeup or..." her voice dropped to a whisper, "whether you have one leg or two. They love you unconditionally. Always."

Her words seemed to suck the conversation right out of the cab. The remainder of the ride was accomplished in silence.

By the time they reached the ranch house, Gavin was ready to leap out of the truck and disappear. Unfortunately, that wasn't the option. He'd brought this woman to Montana. The least he could do was see that she was comfortable until she decided this plan was as ludicrous as he thought it was.

. . .

AURELIA'S GAZE followed the winding road through the trees until it opened into a field with a rise in the center. A sprawling ranch house topped the hill, behind which stood a barn even bigger than the house. There was also a long narrow building and a few smaller ones as well.

As the truck pulled up the drive, a woman with long, straight, sandy-blond hair stepped out onto the porch and shaded her eyes. A man with black hair and dark eyes stepped out behind her and slipped his arm around her waist. She leaned against him and looked up into his eyes with a smile.

Aurelia envied the couple. They appeared at ease with each other and very much in love. As a child, Aurelia had dreamed of that kind of love. Her parents had that kind of love. She'd read about it in the fairy-tales and believed it to be the only love a woman should settle for. Until the full weight of her lineage rested squarely on her shoulders. That had been the day her parents' chauffeur-driven limousine ran off a cliff, killing her parents, her older brother and their driver instantly. The police had deemed it an unfortunate accident. The driver appeared to have lost control of the vehicle, driving too fast on a curvy wet road.

Her heart tugging at the memory, Aurelia swallowed hard on the lump rising in her throat. She missed them terribly. As the only surviving direct descendant of the royal family, everything had fallen on her shoulders. She'd had to arrange the funerals of the chauffeur and the three people she'd loved the most and hold herself together through it all, demonstrating her strength and willingness to continue to guide the country in the new millennium.

All her years growing up, Aurelia had thought her brother would one day be king. He would carry on the family tradition of leading Lastovia. Not her. Not the younger child. She was supposed to have lived outside the media circus, doing what she pleased, traveling the world, exploring and learning about different cultures. She wasn't supposed to be the one stuck making decisions that could affect hundreds of thousands of people. But as the Princess of Lastovia, she could not pursue her dream of roaming the world. Her leaving her country for ten months until her birthday put herself and her reign in jeopardy. But she had to do something drastic in order to comply with Lastovian law.

If she didn't inherit the kingdom, it would be fought over by a couple of her cousins who would be next in the royal lineage. Neither Rupert or Gregory were fit to rule. Both were lazy and too self-centered. They would expect all the trappings without assuming the responsibility. And though the country had established a parliament, her cousins would have far too much access to the royal coffers and bleed the country dry in less than a decade.

As much as Aurelia didn't want the responsibility,

her country was important to her, and she would not see it fall to ruin at the hands of her cousins. If that meant marrying a stranger and begetting heirs to the throne, then she would do whatever it took.

Gavin pulled the truck to a stop, climbed to the ground and made his way to her side. She waited, expecting him to open the door and help her down.

He opened the door, but he didn't extend his hand. Instead, he opened the back door and helped Lori to the ground.

"Thanks," Lori said, adjusting her leg beneath her before releasing his hand. "You should be helping your girl," she said, barely loud enough for Gavin to hear.

Aurelia heard and smiled. "I don't need help," she said and dropped to the ground. Her heels dug into the soft dirt and kept her from moving forward. She swayed and almost fell face-first on the ground.

A big hand shot out, gripped her arm and steadied her. Gavin moved closer, allowing her to rest her body against his.

She swayed even more, but for entirely different reasons. Her knees wobbled, and her heart fluttered at his touch. That had to be a good sign. Then why was she shaking like a frightened kitten?

Fear wasn't what made her shiver. Awareness and desire like none she'd felt before filled every corner of her being. The man was solid. His chest was like steel and his grip strong, like a man who worked with his hands. The thought of those hands working her body made her knees wobble even more.

"Are you okay?" he asked.

She gave him a weak smile. "I shouldn't have worn heels."

He nodded. "You won't have much use for them out here."

"True. A good thing I bought—brought boots." She straightened, pulled her heels out of the soft ground and balanced on the balls of her feet.

"Ready to meet the crew?" Gavin asked, his lips twisting in a wry grin. "They can be a bit over-whelming."

"I'm ready," she said, squared her shoulders and pasted a smile on her face.

First to reach them was the couple from the porch.

"Hi, you must be Aurelia." The sandy-blond-haired woman held out her hand and offered a smile. "I'm Hannah Kendricks. Welcome to Brighter Days Rehab Ranch. So nice to meet you. Any friend of Gavin's has to be pretty awesome. He's been a godsend to us."

Aurelia took the proffered hand and experienced a nice, firm handshake. "Thank you, Hannah. He is pretty special. You're lucky to have him working here."

The man behind Hannah reached around her and

held out his hand. "Alex Davila. My friends call me Taz."

She smiled and shook the man's hand. "I hope to be calling you Taz, soon." And she meant it. The couple seemed open, friendly and genuine. As a royal, Aurelia ran into many people who were nice only because they wanted something from her or the government. These two didn't know who she was, and probably wouldn't care if they did. How refreshing.

Alex leaned close and winked. "You can call him Taz."

A commotion sounded from around the corner of the house. Then two men, each holding one handle of a wheelbarrow, came into view. In the wheelbarrow was another man, with no legs. The two men pushing the wheelbarrow worked in sync, having only one arm each. Behind them came an older man with a shock of gray hair, wearing worn blue jeans and a blue chambray shirt.

The two one-armed men stopped the wheelbarrow just short of where Aurelia stood and tipped it forward. The man inside, set his gloved fists on the earth and levered himself forward. When he stopped, he pulled off a glove and held out his hand. "James Young. You can call me Jimmy. And I believe I'm in love."

Aurelia bent to take his hand, surprised at how strong his grip was. "Pleasure to meet you."

"Please tell me you're single and you're into short men." Jimmy gave her a wide grin.

"Beat it, shorty." The man missing his right arm held out his left hand. "Brody Franklin. Your wish is my command." He bent over her hand and kissed the backs of her knuckles.

"Mr. Franklin." Aurelia tipped her head in acknowledgement, a smile tugging at the corners of her lips.

"Move over, bonehead, let a real man show her how it's done." The dark-haired man missing his left arm lifted her hand. "Xavier Vasquez, *mi amor*. Your beauty outshines the most brilliant star."

Young and Franklin snorted and laughed at the same time.

Gavin stepped between Vasquez and Aurelia. "Back off, guys. She's with me."

All three, limb-challenged men stared at Gavin, eyes wide.

"Blackstock, you been holding out on us?" The older man with the shock of white hair held out his hand to Aurelia. "Don't let these yahoos bother you. If they do, you tell me about it. I'll put them to work mucking the pig pen. Percy Pearson. Ranch foreman." He tipped his head toward Gavin. "How'd a pretty lady like you get mixed up with an old grouch like Blackstock?"

"Before we get into all the details, you might want to meet your new ranch hand." Gavin stepped back and tilted his head toward Collin. "Collin Banner, meet your new bosses, Percy Pearson and Hannah Kendricks. Between the two of them, they run the show around here. Percy's in charge of rehabilitating the animals, while Hannah is in charge of rehabilitating the humans."

"It's a pretty good team," Lori said. "You should like it here. They're doing good things for horses and heroes."

Aurelia's eyebrows shot up. "I'd understood this to be a rehabilitation ranch for military veterans. I didn't realize you were rehabilitating animals, as well."

"Part of helping our veterans is having them care for animals that have been abused or neglected," Hannah said. "By rehabilitating these animals, the humans learn all the things they *can* do, and that what they do makes a difference in an animal's life."

"Have you worked around animals, Banner?" Percy asked.

"Mostly horses," Collin said. "I didn't grow up on a farm or ranch, but my parents scratched enough money together to give me riding lessons. I know one end of a horse from another."

"Good," Percy clapped his hands together. "Those riding skills will come in handy around here. Some places can be difficult to get to in a truck."

Percy turned his attention to Aurelia. "What about you, Miss George?"

"Sir?" She raised her eyebrows.

"Do you ride?" he asked.

Aurelia was pleased she had a little knowledge of animals. Horses, in particular. "I've been riding since I was four." Her parents had been avid horse enthusiasts. She'd even trained in jumping and dressage.

"One thing we like to do as soon as someone comes to stay with us is get them up on a horse," Hannah said. "Something about riding an animal bigger than you is a huge confidence booster."

"Sure is. I've never felt so tall in my life," Young said. "Even when I had legs to stand on."

Aurelia was warmed by the camaraderie amongst the residents and guests of the ranch. For all that these men and women had endured, their outlook and willingness to pitch in was infectious. Aurelia couldn't wait to get started proving herself worthy of this group of people. She had a feeling Gavin would be the hardest to convince.

"Now, if you're done ogling Aurelia, I'm sure she would like to get settled." Gavin grabbed one of Aurelia's suitcases and held out his other hand.

To Aurelia, the gesture was more than just polite. It was, perhaps, the man staking his claim on the woman to all those standing around.

Aurelia took it as a sign that he might be coming around to accepting her as his potential bride. Hope stirred inside her. She laid her hand in his as naturally as if it belonged. The heat and electricity their connection generated made gooseflesh sprout on her arms.

"I'll show Banner to the bunkhouse," Percy offered. "The boys can fill him in on the cleaning duties later. We share the responsibilities, so no one gets stuck doing the dirty work all the time."

Collin nodded. His gaze connected briefly with Aurelia, as if to see if she was all right.

She smiled, reassuringly, her gaze taking in all the people gathered around, so as not to single out Collin.

Gavin tugged on her hand as he started toward the porch.

Aurelia skipped to catch up to his long stride.

"Cookie says dinner will be served in twenty minutes," Hannah called out. She and Taz each grabbed one of Aurelia's two remaining cases and fell in step behind Gavin. "I can show you to your room. The bathroom is across the hall where you can freshen up from your trip."

"Thank you. I don't want to be a burden. Anything I can do to help, I will." Aurelia smiled back at Hannah.

"We're not shy around here. Any help is welcome," Hannah said with a smile. "Cookie has an occasional day off. Can you cook?"

"I don't know; I've never tried." Aurelia said before she remembered she wasn't a princess to these people. Most women and many men in the US could cook.

Aurelia had been surrounded by servants and chefs her entire life. The closest she'd ever come to cooking was when the chef had allowed her to make Christmas cookies one year when she was little. Mostly, she'd been in charge of decorating the cookies with sprinkles.

Taz laughed. "How do you eat, if you don't know how to cook?"

Aurelia scrambled for an answer to his question. "I make sandwiches." The answer was weak at best, but she wasn't lying. On occasion, she'd wandered downstairs in the palace, hungry for a bit to eat. Rather than wake the staff, she'd grabbed bread and slices of whatever meat was available to make sandwiches. That counted, didn't it? She hoped her lack of culinary skills wasn't a deal-breaker with Gavin. Was he old-school and believed women should be responsible for all the cooking and housecleaning? She hoped not, or they'd starve until she learned how.

"Don't worry." Hannah reached out to pat her shoulder. "I'm sure there are plenty of ways you can help, if you want."

"Oh, I want to help. I didn't come here to be waited on," she assured Hannah.

"Good, because we're all pretty busy and could use an extra pair of hands in the house or the barn. You say you know horses?"

She nodded. "I've been around them all my life." Thankfully, another truth.

"Good, we have a couple new rescues who could use some TLC."

Aurelia's brow furrowed. "TLC?"

Hannah grinned. "You really aren't from around here, are you?"

Afraid her ignorance was blowing her cover, Aurelia gave Hannah a shaky smile. "No. I spent a lot of time in Europe. My father was a…diplomat."

Gavin squeezed her hand. "Tender, loving care. TLC."

"Oh, yes. I knew that." Heat rose up her neck and filled her cheeks. "I can do that. I'm very good with horses."

"Then that's where you can help."

"Just don't get too close to the gray mare in the last stall," Gavin warned. "Sassy has yet to calm down. Apparently, whoever had her prior to Brighter Days used a whip on her. She's spooked by practically everything."

Aurelia's chest tightened. "They used a whip on her?"

"Not a riding whip," Gavin said, his lips thinning. "A bull whip. She has the scars across her face to prove it."

"That's awful. They should be whipped." Aurelia clenched her fists. She'd never tolerated people abusing animals. One of her philanthropy projects for her kingdom had been to help establish and fund no-kill shelters for strays. "No one should be cruel to an animal."

"Agreed." Gavin pulled the screen door open and stood back for Aurelia to enter.

She stepped into the dimly lit hallway and paused, blinking to adjust her vision to the shadows after standing in the full light of the sun.

Once she could see, she moved deeper into the entryway, so the others could enter behind her.

The foyer opened into a huge living room with leather chairs and couches and a massive stone fireplace. A broad staircase led to an upper level.

Gavin moved aside, allowing Hannah to climb the steps ahead of them. She led the way to a room on the right side of the hallway. As she passed the door before it, she tapped the wood paneling. "This is Gavin's room. You'll be next to him. Taz and I are at the end of the hall. Lori's room is in the wing on the other side of the staircase." She pushed into the bedroom one door farther down the hallway. Inside was a queen-size bed made of white iron with a lovely, handmade quilt and a white, frothy bed skirt.

Taz and Hannah set the two smaller cases inside the door to Aurelia's room.

Gavin set her larger suitcase on the floor at the end of the bed. "If you need me, I'll be in the next room," he said, and backed through the door.

"Extra towels are in the bathroom, and if you need another blanket, there's one in the closet."

Hannah smiled. "Welcome to Brighter Days. We're glad you came." The pretty owner left the room and closed the door behind her, leaving Aurelia alone for the first time since she'd boarded the plane leaving her country.

Aurelia stood for a long moment, remembering how to breathe, a thousand thoughts swirling through her head. The one rising to the top was that these people had opened their home, arms and lives to her. And she was using them. Using Gavin to get what she wanted. Suddenly, all her plans seemed less clear, less noble. Her country was important to her. But she imagined Gavin's was important to him. He'd sacrificed himself to protect the freedoms of his people. What would she give him in return for marrying her and giving her a baby? How willing would he be to leave Montana for a foreign country? He'd have to love someone very much to give up all of this.

She had to tell him the truth. But when? Before they got to know each other? Before he had the chance to get to know her for herself, not as the princess of a small country.

The weight of her decisions bore down on her shoulders, and exhaustion threatened to make things worse. She'd have time to tell Gavin, and she would... after they had a chance to get to know each other.

Squaring her shoulders, opened her suitcase and pulled out the new jeans and soft blue chambray shirts she'd selected to work in. If Gavin was going to see her as worthy of marrying, she'd have to prove she could pull her weight amongst these motivated veterans.

Hell, she'd even learn to cook, if she didn't burn down the house first.

CHAPTER 5

GAVIN RETREATED TO HIS ROOM, where he paced the floor softly, listening to every sound emanating from the room next door. So far, he heard nothing but what he assumed was a zipper sliding around the outside of her suitcase. Since then, nothing.

He could still feel the heat of her hand in his and the fire it had ignited through his veins. What was happening to him? She was a stranger. All he knew about her was what she'd told him in her on-line questionnaire. He'd contacted his friend Hank Patterson, the head of Brotherhood Protectors as soon as he'd learned Aurelia was coming. Hank had promised to do what he could.

Gavin pulled out his cell phone and dialed Hank's number.

"Blackstock, I was about to call," Hank answered. "Did she arrive?"

"She's here," Gavin said softly, not wanting his voice to carry through the walls to Aurelia.

"I still don't understand why you want to do a background check on someone you know. However, I worked with a buddy of mine in the FBI. He ran a check on the woman's name and Maine address. The address is legit, but it belongs to a Sean O'Bannon, not Aurelia George."

"Could she be renting from him?"

"Without going to Maine and checking for myself," Hank said, "I couldn't tell you that."

"Anything else?" Gavin asked, his gut twisting.

"The good news is, she doesn't have a police record," Hank offered.

That only meant she hadn't gotten caught at anything, yet. "Thanks, Hank."

"I thought you knew this woman. Why are you running a background check on her?"

"Call me jaded, but I didn't want to bring anyone to Brighter Days Ranch I hadn't had checked out. I can't remember the last time we met, and online communication is sketchy at best." Because they hadn't. Gavin hated lying to Hank, but he wasn't ready to reveal how he'd met Aurelia. Frankly, he was embarrassed he'd sunk that low as to send for a mail-order bride.

"One other thing," Hank said. "She's not registered anywhere we could find for a driver's license."

"No driver's license?" Gavin shoved a hand

through his hair. "Who doesn't have a driver's license in this day and age?"

"Usually people who live in big cities and use mass transit to get around," Hank said.

"But the address she listed was in Maine."

"She could have lived there at one time, but might be living in a city...? Sounds like she has some explaining to do."

"When I get her alone, I'll fill in the blanks." And he would. He prayed she wasn't all bad news and planning on stealing from Hannah. Or killing them all in their sleep.

Shit. What had he done?

Gavin stopped himself short of marching into the room next door and demanding all the answers. There was too much he didn't know about her.

When she'd stepped off that bus... Damn, he'd fallen under her spell. The woman was even more beautiful than he'd expected. Which made Gavin even more suspicious.

Why would a gorgeous woman resort to a mail-order bride website to land a husband? Aurelia could have any man she wanted. Why a broken-down veteran? He didn't have a lot of money, just some savings he'd held onto with the intention of eventually buying a piece of land and building a house. That was before he'd lost his leg. Lately, it hadn't seemed worth the effort, if he didn't have someone to share it with.

He might as well continue to work at Brighter Days. At least, he wouldn't be alone.

Unless, by some miracle, this mail-order bride thing managed to work out.

Gavin shook his head. No way. There had to be a catch. Beautiful women didn't put themselves up on sites like that without a reason.

He left his room and stood in the hallway, waiting for Aurelia to open her door. When she did, he'd demand to know the answers to all his questions. And a search of her suitcases might be a good idea as well. What if she were hiding a gun or a knife amid her lace panties? He couldn't live with himself if something awful happened to Hannah or anyone else at the ranch.

After several minutes, he couldn't wait any longer.

He knocked.

The doorknob turned, causing Gavin's breath to lodge in his throat.

When the door opened, he charged forward, pushing it and Aurelia back into the bedroom.

Her eyes wide, she stepped back. "What's wrong?"

"This whole idea. I know nothing about you. Nothing. And I've invited you onto the Brighter Day's Ranch not knowing why you're here." He spoke softly, so as not to alert others in the house. "You could be a killer, waiting to slit our throats, or a thief planning on stealing anything of value in the night.

How do I know you won't hurt the people I care about here?"

Aurelia's hands came up in a surrendering gesture. She'd changed out of the dress and high heels she'd arrived in and now wore jeans and a soft blue shirt, and her feet were bare. The outfit made her look more girl-next-door, younger and more vulnerable. "I'm sorry you feel this way. Perhaps this would work out better if I stayed at a hotel in town until we got to know each other better." She shook her head. "I had no intention of doing any of those things, but you have no reason to believe me." Aurelia turned to her suitcase. "You can search my suitcases and this room, if it makes you feel better." She flung open the large suitcase and tossed its contents onto the quilt.

"You see? I don't have anything stashed in my clothes." When she'd emptied the contents, she stood back. "You can check the lining. I have nothing to hide. Look in the other cases, too. Even if I had a gun, I've never fired one. I wouldn't know how. As for knives... I don't like the sight of blood. I don't need money. But you're right." She piled her clothing back into her suitcase. "You don't know me. I could be a thief or a killer, for all you know. I think it would be better if I stayed in town." She tossed in the dress and the high heels she'd been wearing when she'd arrived and zipped the suitcase. "I'll need a ride into town." She straightened, her chin held high. "I'm sorry I've caused you so much discomfort. That was not my intention."

As he stood in front of her, Gavin felt like a fool. The woman had put herself out there, coming from as far away as Maine to meet a stranger. For all she knew, he could have been the killer, the thief or worse. He could have lured her all the way to Montana to sell her into the sex trade.

Gavin shoved a hand through his hair. "No. No. I...I don't think you need to stay in town. Besides, Eagle Rock is not large enough for a hotel. The best we can do is a bed and breakfast or a room over the Blue Moose Tavern. And that's too noisy." He shook his head. "It's just..."

"You don't know me."

"And the same can be said for you...about me."

Aurelia smiled. "True." She held out her hand. "Hello, I'm Aurelia S-George. Nice to meet you."

Gavin gripped her hand in his. "I'm sorry to be so suspicious."

"And I wish we could have met under better circumstances. But sometimes, meeting people can be difficult, and we have to resort to the internet." Aurelia squeezed his hand. "If you want to call this whole idea off, I will understand. We gave each other the option to back out, if we didn't feel we were right for each other. I'll honor that agreement, no hard feelings."

The longer he held her hand, the more he wanted

to keep holding it. "I don't want you to move into town."

Her lips twitched on the corners. "Would it help if I promise not to murder you in your sleep?"

He felt his own lips quirk at her words. "That would do for a start."

"You're next door to me. I'm sure you can hear me moving about. If you want, I can promise to be with you whenever I'm not in my room or in the bathroom. That way you can keep an eye on me until you're more comfortable with my intentions. I'm really only here for the same reason you wanted me here. I want to be married. I want children."

"Why me?" Gavin blurted out. And since he'd started it, he couldn't stop. "You're a beautiful woman. You could have anyone you want. Why would you want to marry a medically retired military guy with one leg? You could do so much better."

"Don't sell yourself short. You're a handsome man. I was drawn to your picture on the internet. And the fact you're former military is an added plus. I know you're disciplined, and you can take care of yourself in any given situation." She nodded toward his prosthetic leg. "The fact you're missing a leg but are still highly functional and living a normal life is proof you can take care of yourself and any wife and children who come along." She flung out her arm. "So many of the men I meet aren't capable of fending for themselves. And they don't see me as a person, but as an asset like an accessory to their clothing or only as a beautiful woman incapable of intelligent thought, conversation or usefulness."

"What makes you think I don't think the same?" Gavin challenged.

"You advertised for a woman willing to work hard and bear children. I took that as someone who would work alongside you. As an equal."

"More than an equal. Call me selfish, but I want a family," Gavin said. "And you can do what I can't... bear children."

She tipped her head. "True. But I can't and won't have children without a husband to give them a name and to help see to their safety." Aurelia lifted her chin. "And if we get along well and learn to care for each other, that would be an added bonus."

Gavin frowned. "But it's not a deal-breaker?"

She shook her head. "Sometimes deep respect is a better foundation for a long-lasting relationship. Too often, after the lust wears off, a couple doesn't have anything else in common."

Gavin drew in a deep breath and let it go. "You're so young to be so jaded."

"I'll be thirty in less than a year." She gave him half of a smile. "I guess I've seen the best and worst in people."

"And that's why you chose this route instead of dating and falling in love?"

"As I said, I'll be thirty in less than year, and I feel

my biological clock ticking. I've known women who chose their career first and waited until they were in their thirties to have children, only to find that they'd waited too long. Their eggs had dried up, or something like that. They were unable to get pregnant." Aurelia lifted her chin. "I want children. I never considered living my life without ever being a mother."

"And though I went through the mail-order bride site, I guess I never considered living my life without someone to love," Gavin said softly. He laughed, the sound harsh to his own ears. "But then, I never imagined I'd lose a leg. That tends to change a few things. And here we are."

Aurelia's gaze locked with Gavin's. For a long moment, neither said anything.

Finally, Aurelia broke the silence. "So, do we end this now? If you give me a ride back to the bus station, I'll catch the next bus out of here."

"The next bus out isn't until Tuesday."

"Then I'll stay at the bed and breakfast or the tavern."

Gavin shook his head. "No. You're staying here."

She frowned. "Until Tuesday? Or are you saying you're willing to give this insanity a shot?"

"I'm willing to give it one day at a time."

She nodded. "Fair enough." Aurelia looked away, licking her lips. "Should we at least see if we're compatible?"

"I thought that's what I meant by taking it one day at a time."

Aurelia's lips curled into a small smile. "I meant, shall we see if we have any chemistry?"

Gavin's eyes narrowed. Every time he'd touched her, he'd felt something. Was it chemistry? He didn't know, but it burned through him like lightning. "What do you suggest?"

Again, she looked away. "A kiss?" She went on, speaking fast. "It doesn't have to be anything earth-shattering, but it might let us know if there's any chance of making this more than a marriage of convenience. But if you don't want to, or you think it's too soon—"

Pulling her into his arms, Gavin pressed his lips to hers in a light kiss, afraid he'd scare her if he did what he really wanted to do. "Like that?"

Aurelia's eyes closed, and she pressed her lips together as if testing them. "I'm not sure."

"It didn't do anything for you, did it?"

She sighed. "No."

Before he could reason away his next move, he yanked her against his chest and claimed her mouth, in a crushing kiss. He skimmed the seam of her lips with his tongue.

When she opened to him, he swept in and caressed the length of her tongue in a long, sensuous move that left him hot and breathless.

Her arms circled the back of his neck, dragging

him closer.

He slid his hands down to the small of her back and pressed her hips against his, the evidence of his desire pressing into her belly.

When he finally brought up his head, he dragged in a ragged breath and let it out slowly.

Aurelia leaned her forehead against his chest, her fingers curling into his shirt.

"Well?" he said, his voice a little on the shaky side. "Was that better?"

She nodded, her head bumping against his chest. "Much."

"I'm game to give it another day if you are," he said, his voice a little hoarse.

Her shoulders rose and fell on a deep breath, and she looked up. "I'm game."

"Then I'll leave you to finish getting ready. We can walk down to the dining room together, if you'd like."

"I'd like that," she said.

Gavin left the room and closed the door behind him, feeling as if he'd been sucker-punched in the gut. That kiss had done more than get better. It had rocked his world so completely, he couldn't see straight, much less think. He'd gone into that room ready to kick the woman out of the house, off the ranch and out of his world. When he'd come out, he began counting the seconds until he saw her again. And prayed he'd get another chance to kiss her.

Soon.

CHAPTER 6

AURELIA LEANED her cheek against the cool paneling of the door, willing the heat to abate. Her lips still tingled, and her insides roiled with a warm wave of desire. What had just happened? She'd come to Montana to marry and have a baby by her thirtieth birthday, not to fall for the man. Of course, that would be a bonus, but not all royal weddings had to be for love.

The inherited obligation to produce an heir was the primary goal for marrying. That had been her brother's legacy. Until he and her parents died in a car crash.

Her parents had been for the intelligence and good sense of the other. After producing two children and raising them to inherit the kingdom, they'd finally found a deep, lasting love and time to spend together.

Along with exploring the world, Aurelia had dreamed of falling in love and marrying the man of her dreams. Now, she only hoped to marry and have the child that would save the kingdom from his rule.

But that kiss... Sweet Jesus.

That kiss filled her foolish heart with hope for a happily-ever-after, a chance at love and a life with a husband and family. She'd kissed boys as a school girl, and men when dating and had even made love, but never, had anything made her feel the barrage of sensations she'd experienced kissing Gavin.

The connection had left her weak in the knees and unable to catch her breath. And it must have made an impression on him because he was willing to give their insane proposal another day.

More than ever before, Aurelia felt this was her only chance. If she wanted to keep her family legacy intact, she had only a couple of weeks to convince Gavin their marriage was the right thing to do.

After the kiss, the thought of making babies had taken on an entirely different context. Having sex with Gavin Blackstock would not be a hardship. If he made love half as expertly as he kissed...

Aurelia fanned herself, the heat spreading throughout her body, pooling at her core. She had to get out there and make him see that they had a chance at a life together, or there wouldn't be sex with Gavin, or a wedding or a child by her thirtieth birthday.

Aurelia slipped socks on her feet and pushed her feet into the pair of dingo boots the salesman had assured her were the right kind of boot to wear on a ranch. They were surprisingly comfortable. After tucking her shirt into her jeans and slipping a leather belt through the loops, Aurelia pulled her long, blond hair back into a ponytail and left her room.

As promised, Gavin waited for her on the landing. He held out his hand, not his arm, and clasped her hand inside his. Together, they walked down the stairs and into the kitchen.

Hannah stood in the middle of the large kitchen filled with the wonderful smells of food. "We could use the dining room, but the table in here is plenty big, and the hands are used to eating in here."

"Formal dining rooms are for weddings and funerals," Percy said. "I prefer eating in the kitchen where Cookie makes the magic happen."

"Thanks, Percy." A short man with thick arms, close-cropped brown hair and green eyes, pushed his sleeves up past his elbows. "You might not think it's magic when you discover we're having beef stew and cornbread for dinner."

Percy grinned and rubbed his belly. "Pure magic, my friend. Pure magic. They taught you well in the Air Force."

Cookie snorted. "Never set foot in a kitchen on active duty. Learned it all when I retired."

Aurelia's chest swelled with hope. If Cookie could learn to cook later in life, so could she.

The entire crew was gathered around a large wooden table. In the center of the table were platters of fluffy yellow cornbread, two large tureens of steaming stew and pitchers of iced tea.

Gavin held Aurelia's chair as she took her seat. Then he sat beside her.

The others pulled out chairs and filled in around the massive table. Lori sat across from Aurelia. Taz and Hannah sat at the head and foot of the table, respectively. Cookie brought over a couple of large ladles for the stew and took a seat at the table.

In the palace, the cook never ate with the royal family. Nor did the staff or stable hands. Aurelia liked the feeling that everyone in the room was part of one big family.

Used to having staff serve the food, Aurelia sat back and watched as everyone reached for the food, passed it down and helped each other serve portions into their bowls and onto their plates. They attacked the hearty stew with gusto and bit into chunks of the cake-like cornbread. Having never encountered cornbread, Aurelia wasn't quite sure how to eat it.

"Have you never eaten cornbread?" Gavin asked.

Aurelia shook her head, hoping cornbread was not normally served in Maine.

"Some folks consider cornbread a southern food. Cookie is from Louisiana. So, you'll see some of the southern influence in his menus," Hannah said. "I particularly love his gumbo and dirty rice."

Gavin leaned close to Aurelia. "Some people like butter on their cornbread. Others like it with jelly. Me? I prefer honey." He lifted a jar from the middle of the table and poured thick honey over his cornbread. Then he offered the jar to Aurelia and served a wedge of cornbread onto her plate.

Following his example, she poured honey onto the corner of the bread. Using her fork, she dug into the corner and lifted it up into her mouth. The combination of the cakelike bread and the honey melted in her mouth.

"Like that?" Gavin asked.

She nodded, poured more honey and took another bite.

"I like to dip my cornbread into my stew." Lori picked up the entire slice of cornbread and dipped the end into her stew.

Thinking it couldn't get better than honey, Aurelia gave it a try anyway. Instead of sticky sweet, the cornbread came out with the hot, savory stew covering it. When she placed it in her mouth, it became an explosion of flavor on her tongue. She hadn't realized how hungry she was.

Collin sat at the other end of the table, eating like he was indulging in his last meal. He was probably happy to be back in the states, eating more familiar foods.

"How's the stew and cornbread?" Cookie asked.

Aurelia smiled at the older man. "Wonderful," she said.

"Save some room for strawberry rhubarb pie," Cookie said. "I made three."

"Cookie, Aurelia has never cooked," Hannah said. "I bet she'd like to learn. Could you give her a few pointers?"

"Sure. Any time," Cookie said.

"Aurelia, how long will you be with us?" Hannah asked.

With a quick glance at Gavin, Aurelia shrugged. She wanted to stay as long as it took, but she wouldn't pressure Gavin, even though her time was dwindling down. "I don't know. Hopefully, long enough to help out around here."

"Won't your family miss you?" Hannah asked and then popped a spoonful of stew into her mouth.

Aurelia's chest squeezed tightly. Though it had been over two years, she still couldn't wrap her mind around the fact they were gone. She shook her head, her gaze going to the stew in the bowl in front of her. "I don't have any immediate family left."

Hannah frowned. "I'm sorry to hear that. When my mother died of cancer, I thought I was alone in the world. It's the worst feeling ever."

"Hey, you had me," Gavin said. "Friends are like family."

"Yes, I did, and yes, they are," Hannah said. "And then I learned who my father was."

"And now she has me." Taz winked at Hannah across the table.

Hannah smiled. "I still miss my mother, but it does help having people you love around you." She tilted her head to the side. "Do you mind if I ask what happened to your family?"

When Aurelia hesitated, Hannah held up her hand. "Don't answer, if it's too painful."

Aurelia drew in a deep breath and let it out slowly. "My parents and my older brother were killed when their car ran off the road two years ago."

"I'm sorry," Hannah said. "I don't know which is worse, losing someone so fast, or watching a loved one suffer until they finally pass. At least, I got to say my goodbyes before my mother died."

"Could we talk about something more cheerful?" Young lifted his tea glass. "I'd like to propose a toast to new friends who like horses." He lifted his glass toward Collin and then Aurelia. "To Collin and Miss George. Welcome to Brighter Days."

Everyone around the table raised a glass to the two new residents. "To Collin and Miss George," they said in unison.

Heat filled Aurelia's cheeks. "Thank you, but you must call me Aurelia. Miss George is too formal."

"Done," Young said and set his glass on the table.

"Cookie, I think Aurelia might like some of that pie now."

"We'll get them." Franklin and Vasquez said as one, and then leaped to their feet and rushed to the counter where the pies sat cooling. They brought two of the pies back to the table. Then Franklin returned to the counter for the third pie, and Vasquez went for dessert plates and a knife.

Talk turned to the newest rescues at the ranch.

"I'm worried about Sassy," Percy said. "She kicks at her stall. I'm afraid she'll hurt herself."

"And when we let her out in the paddock, it's hard to get her back in the stall," Franklin said.

"She needs to get used to the stall. It gets too cold in the winter for her to be outside," Hannah said.

"I suspect she was left out all winter with her last owner." Percy shook his head. "The cattle survive in subzero temperatures and wild horses do as well. I'm more concerned about damage to her legs."

"The neighbors who turned in Sassy's owner for abuse said they think she came from a farm back east. They think she was trained in dressage or jumping." Gavin cut a slice of pie out and laid it on a dessert plate and then passed it to Aurelia. "The man who bought her only wanted her to use as a cutting horse. Apparently, she didn't respond well to his training techniques."

"Using a bull whip isn't a training technique,"

Aurelia muttered, appalled anyone would do that to a horse.

"Agreed." Hannah took a bite of the pie and smiled. "Cookie, you outdid yourself. This is so good."

Aurelia bit into the slice of pie Gavin had served her and smiled. "This is very good. Bravo to the chef."

Everyone around the table laughed.

Aurelia blinked. "What? Did I say something wrong?"

"Not at all," Hannah chuckled. "It's just that Cookie doesn't consider himself a chef. Isn't that right?"

Cookie nodded. "I think of the kitchen like a stationary chuck wagon. Simple victuals that are filling and healthy. I don't do those fancy meals."

"But what you do is delicious," Aurelia said. "Thank you."

Dinner wrapped up with the guys raucous laughter and everyone helping carry dishes and platters to the sink and counter.

"I'll wash," Gavin offered.

"Why don't you show Aurelia how beautiful the Montana sunsets can be?" Hannah took the plate from Gavin's hand.

"Please," Aurelia said. "I'd like to help." She'd never washed a dish in her life, but it couldn't be that hard.

Lori took the plate from Aurelia's hand. "First

night, you get a pass on dishes. Go. The sunsets are amazing."

Aurelia gave Gavin a weak smile. "I guess we've been voted out of the kitchen."

He held out his hand, as it seemed to be his habit.

As easily as breathing, Aurelia slipped her palm against his. His fingers curled around hers, warm and strong. She liked how safe and protected it made her feel.

"We'll take care of the animals," Franklin offered.

"Hey, speak for yourself," Vasquez punched Franklin in his good arm.

"Fine. I'll take care of the animals," the blond-haired, green-eyed young man said. "They like me better, anyway."

"The hell they do," Vasquez said. He raced Franklin to the back door, both hitting the frame as they tried to squeeze through at the same time.

"Those two will never grow up," Young said. He levered himself out of his wheelchair and, using his arms, propelled himself to the door. "I'll just go supervise to keep them from starting World War III."

"Hannah and I will clean up the kitchen," Taz said.

"I'll wash," Hannah said. "Cookie, grab a beer and put your feet up. Your duty is done in here."

Gavin led Aurelia out the back door and eased himself down onto the top of the steps, stretching a stiff leg out in front of him. He patted the board beside him.

Aurelia dropped down and onto the step. The sun had slipped low in the sky, cresting the top of a snow-covered peak. "Do the mountains have snow on them year-round?"

"Sometimes," Gavin said "We haven't had that hot a summer, and we had a late snow. We've had snow in July in the upper elevations."

The bright orange blob dipped halfway below the highest peak, spreading purple, mauve and blue hues through the clouds hugging the mountaintops.

"Hannah was right," Aurelia said, her voice hushed in the face of nature's majesty. "The sunset is remarkable."

Without the warming rays spilling over them, the heat dispersed and cool night air settled over the ranch.

Aurelia shivered.

"It gets quite cool out here at night. We should get you inside." Gavin started to rise.

"I'm okay. I want to take in the full effect of the sunset, the scents of the evergreens and the sound of the horses whinnying. I don't think I've been to a place so peaceful." She couldn't help another shiver.

Gavin slipped an arm around her. "Really, we should go in."

Aurelia snuggled closer to the man, absorbing the heat of his body. "I'm fine, now. Your body is like a heater."

"Takes a lot cooler weather to make me cold. And,

believe me, it gets a lot colder here in the winter time."

"I've read that the jet stream dips low through here, driving temperatures into the negatives."

"True. And if the wind is blowing, it cuts through you, no matter how many layers you wear." He tightened his hold on her as if protecting her from the effects of the wind.

"Do you have to go out in the cold?"

"As long as there are animals, we go out. We bring the cattle closer to the barn in the winter and feed them hay. Most of the horses can survive the cold, but we bring in the weak, the little ones and the old."

"I thought Brighter Days Rehabilitation Ranch was for veterans. But it's more than that, isn't it?"

"Like Hannah said, we take in neglected, unwanted or abused horses and help them thrive."

"It's a noble undertaking. And from what I've seen, it seems to work well with the veterans. The guests here are well-adjusted and thriving."

"And the animals are doing well due to their care and treatment by our veterans."

"So, are you one of the guests?"

He rubbed the top of his bum leg. "I'm not a guest. I'm somewhat of a permanent fixture here. Hannah and I go way back. We grew up here in Eagle Rock. We've been friends since I can remember. When I came back from the war injured, she decided it was her calling in life to do what she could for me and other soldiers, sailors, airmen and marines who have suffered from having deployed. Some have come through here with physical challenges, others have had the emotional challenges of fitting back into the civilian world after the fast pace, danger and trauma of war. They're welcome here, and Hannah works as a therapist to help them through their issues."

"And you?"

"Mostly, I help Percy and teach the guys what it means to run a ranch and care for animals. I'm pretty good at fixing things that are broke, and I'm handy with a hammer and nails."

"Is this where you plan to stay for the rest of your life?"

"I don't know. I once thought I'd have a piece of land of my own. Maybe build a house and raise cattle and horses."

"And you don't want that now?"

He shrugged. "Things changed."

"You think you can't do all that now that you've lost a leg?"

He tensed against her. "At first, I thought that."

"And now?"

"I know I can do whatever I set my mind to. Thanks to Hannah and Brighter Days."

"Will Montana always be your home?" Aurelia closed her eyes and inhaled the scent of the trees and the man beside her. Would a man like Gavin leave the beauty of this country to follow her back to Lastovia? Could she dare to dream?

He shrugged again. "It has always been my home."

"Have you ever thought of living anywhere else?" she whispered.

Gavin leaned away from her to let him stare down into her eyes. "You haven't been here twenty-four hours and you already want to leave?"

She smiled. "No. I want to stay. For a while."

His lips twisted. "These people and this place haven't made you want to run screaming?"

"Actually, I'm impressed and endeared by the residents of Brighter Days. They give me hope for the future."

"Wait until you see how hard we work around here. You might change your mind." He ran his gaze over her. "I get the feeling you haven't worked on a ranch before."

She nodded. "You're right. But I'm ready and willing."

"You don't have to, you know."

"That was part of the advertisement. I'm willing to work hard." She didn't add *and bear children,* the other part of the deal.

Based on the look in Gavin's eyes, he was thinking of that promise as well.

"I'm committed to this union." She stared directly into his eyes. "I'm not afraid." She slipped her hand into his and squeezed.

Gavin looked down at where their hands joined. "I haven't married for a reason."

"And that reason is...?"

"When I was on active duty, I didn't think it fair to put a woman through the worry of wondering if her husband, the father of her children, would come home in one piece or in a body bag."

Aurelia's chest tightened.

"And I didn't want to burden a woman with a shell of a man, should I return home in pieces." He looked up and captured her gaze. "When I returned home in pieces, like I'd feared, I thought my chances at a normal life were over."

"What changed your mind?"

He looked around at the ranch shadowed in dusk. "This place. Hannah. Percy. Lori. Franklin, Vasquez and Young." A chuckle rumbled out of his chest. "While I was trying to keep it together for them, they showed me hope and proved to me I'm still capable of living a full life."

"Then why did you feel it necessary to apply to a mail-order bride site?" Aurelia asked.

"I know I'm capable. Convincing a woman that a one-legged cowboy is a safe bet... Well, the odds were against me."

"You sell yourself short." Aurelia cupped his chin. "You're a handsome man, with or without the leg. You could have any woman you want with the crook of your finger."

Gavin snorted. "Look where I live. The back-woods of Montana aren't full of willing women."

She smiled. "You got me here."

"Because of a wild idea and a push from a friend." He brushed a strand of her hair back from her cheek.

"Any regrets, so far?" she whispered.

His lips twitched. "As long as you don't slit my throat in my sleep, I'm good."

"I won't slit it." She pressed her lips to his throat. "Though, I might kiss it." She couldn't resist. They were sitting so closely. He smelled of man and the outdoors, an intoxicating scent. Aurelia leaned closer, daring to dream this crazy scheme might just work. He was the real deal. A man who cared about others.

All she wanted at that moment was to kiss him.

With his thumb and forefinger, Gavin tipped her chin. "If we were deciding based on chemistry, this would be a no-brainer." He lowered his head and brushed his lips across hers.

"No-brainer," she whispered and met his lips with her own.

"Help! Percy! Hannah! Someone! Help!" a shout sounded from the direction of the barn.

Gavin's head jerked up.

The piercing scream of a horse followed the shout and the sound of frantic banging against wood.

Gavin pushed to his feet, pulling Aurelia up with him.

"Help!" The shout came again.

Gavin ran down the remaining steps and across the yard toward the barn, shouting over his shoulder. "Stay here."

Aurelia refused to stand by while someone needed assistance. She ran after Gavin, following him into the barn where chaos reigned.

CHAPTER 7

GAVIN RAN INTO THE BARN, his heart pounding, his gaze shooting around the dimly lit interior.

Loud banging and a horse's frantic scream sounded from the far right corner.

"We gotta get him out of there," Franklin tugged on the stall door. "I can't get this to open."

"Get who out?" Gavin demanded as he ran toward the younger man.

"Vasquez went in to get the feed bucket. Sassy went ape-shit crazy."

Gavin raced to the stall door. "Get back."

"You gotta get him out of there," Franklin said as he backed away.

Gavin pulled at the sliding lever, but it wouldn't budge.

A moan sounded from the other side of door, spurring Gavin to try harder. He pushed against the wood panel and pulled at the lever at the same time. It moved an inch. He shoved harder on the stall door.

The metal lever released, and the door slid open

The gray mare, eyes rolled back in her head, lunged through the opening, knocking Gavin to the ground.

He rolled to the side and pushed up on his good foot.

Inside the stall, Vasquez huddled in a tight ball in the corner, the feed bucket in front of him. He had a cut on his forehead, and he stared up at Gavin. "About time you showed up," he said, his voice shaking.

Gavin leaned over the younger man. "Where are you hurt?"

"She reared and clipped me in the head. I fell but managed to get into the corner before she started kicking the shit out of the stall. That horse is crazy."

Gavin held out a hand to Vasquez. "Grab my hand if you're up to standing."

Vasquez placed his hand in Gavin's and let him pull him to his feet. He swayed but managed to remain upright.

"We should get you to a doctor. You could be suffering from a concussion."

"Miss George, don't you go near that horse. She's spooked," Franklin called from the other side of the stall.

"Damn," Gavin released Vasquez's hand and dove for the stall door.

On the other side of the barn, Aurelia inched toward Sassy, speaking in a slow, even tone. She held out her hand, her palm up, never slowing the singsong sound of her words.

"You're a beauty, Miss Sassy. A lovely, magnificent animal with fire in your soul and determination in your heart. Someone hurt you, made you afraid. But I won't hurt you. I'll be your friend. I'll brush you and bring you treats. Do you like carrots or apples? I bet I can find some for you. Would you like that? No one is going to whip you ever again. These people only want to help you and make your life so much better." As she spoke, she moved closer to the animal.

Sassy's eyes were wide, the whites showing in her fear. She danced backward until her hindquarters bumped into the wall. But she didn't rear, and she didn't kick. Instead, she pawed the ground in front of her and nickered nervously.

"I'm not going to hurt you," Aurelia said. She stood so close that if the horse decided to rear, she'd be trampled in a second.

Gavin's breath caught in his throat.

"That horse will kill her," Young said as he came to rest beside Franklin. "Do something."

"We can't. Aurelia is too close. If we move," Gavin whispered, "we could startle Sassy and make her lash out."

"We can't just stand here and do nothing..." Franklin said softly and started forward.

Gavin gripped the man's shoulder and held him in place. "We can if we don't want Aurelia hurt."

Wishing he could do more, Gavin stood back and let Aurelia work her magic, praying the horse didn't see her as a threat and trample her into the ground.

"Sweet Sassy, you're a very misunderstood creature. All you want is to run free and dance in the wind. Don't we all? Come to me. I promise to feed you sweet treats and scratch behind your ears. You and I will be great friends. You'll see." Aurelia reached for the mare's halter.

Gavin leaned forward, ready to race to Aurelia's side, but he didn't need to.

Sassy tossed her head but didn't fight Aurelia's hold on the halter. After several more tosses, the horse calmed and let the woman rub her hand over the velvet-soft nose.

"You're not so bad when you're handled like the lady you are," Aurelia murmured. "You just need some TLC. And I'll give you all you need. Yes, my darling. You will be loved and cared for here."

Aurelia held onto the halter and ran her hand along the horse's jaw and up to scratch behind her ears.

"I'll be damned," Vasquez said. "She's got that horse mesmerized."

"She's doing a good job on me, too," Young said. "She'd have me eating out of her hand."

Gavin stepped toward Aurelia and Sassy. As he neared, Sassy jerked her head up, her eyes rolling back.

"Don't come closer," Aurelia warned in a soft voice. "I've got her. I think she might be spooked by men."

"That would make sense, since her previous owner was a male and he whipped her."

"Do we know who her owner was before the jerk who abused her?" Aurelia asked, smoothing her hand over Sassy's neck, her tone still soft and musical.

"The neighbor thinks she belonged to a young woman who died of cancer. Her family sold the horse to help pay the medical bills.

"Oh, how sad. To lose the person you love and be sold to a callous, evil man." Aurelia leaned her forehead against the horse's forehead. "You don't even know what you did wrong to deserve that kind of treatment. And you probably miss your lady."

Gavin shook his head. Aurelia knew exactly what the mare needed. And the horse responded in kind.

Aurelia held her hand out behind her. "I'd really like a lead, if that's possible."

Gavin grabbed one hanging on a nail and eased toward her, ducking low to keep from spooking the mare.

Once he laid the rope in her hand, he backed away and let Aurelia snap the lead onto Sassy's halter.

"Open the door to the barn," Aurelia instructed.

"She might run away," Franklin warned. "We struggled to get her into the barn in the first place."

"I'll take my chances," Aurelia murmured softly, rubbing Sassy's neck.

"Let go if she does try to make a run for it," Gavin urged. "Don't get your hand caught in the lead."

"I've led a high-spirited horse before. I know how to handle one," Aurelia assured him. "Please, open the door."

Gavin moved toward the center barn door and slid it to the side.

Sassy danced sideways and whinnied.

Aurelia held the lead firmly in her left hand, maintaining control with her right hand on the halter. She walked steadily and quietly to the door.

Once outside in the gathering dusk, she led the mare around the barnyard, making several circular passes before she returned to the barn door. She led her in through the opening and into the stall.

Franklin shook his head. "You'd never believe that was the same animal of a few minutes ago."

"Mesmerized," Young said. "I think I'm in love."

"With the horse?" Franklin said.

"No, asshole, with the girl," Young said and punched Franklin in the knee.

Franklin hopped to the side, out of Young's reach. "Hey, that's hitting a guy below the belt."

"Just be glad I didn't aim higher," Young said. He turned to Gavin. "She's going to be great with Sassy. Why didn't we think of Sassy being afraid of men?"

"Because we don't think like a female, *dufus*," Franklin said. "Aurelia has it right. Until Sassy realizes all men aren't assholes, we'll have one of the females take care of her."

Aurelia crooned to the mare inside the stall and emerged a moment later, carrying the bucket and the lead. "I'll get her feed, if you point me in the right direction."

Gavin slid the stall door shut behind Aurelia and led her to the grain bins. He reached for the bucket, but she held it away.

"Willing to work hard was one of the requirements." She smiled up at him. "I might not know how to cook but let me prove myself around the horses."

Gavin dipped his head. "Fair enough. I'd say you've more than proven yourself. But you scared the fool out of all of us in the process."

Her eyes widened. "I did?" She glanced at the others standing nearby.

Franklin, Young and Vasquez all nodded in unison.

"You did," Young voiced their thoughts.

"So, please, don't put yourself in harm's way again," Gavin said. "I can't afford anymore gray hairs."

Aurelia snorted. "You don't have any gray hairs."

"Sadly, I do. I found one just this morning." He pointed to the top of his head. "I'm not getting any younger, and witnessing you walking up to a wild-eyed horse didn't help in that department."

"You'll be even more handsome with gray hair. Poor Sassy was in a state. I couldn't leave her to fret."

"A state?" Vasquez's brows twisted.

"Fret?" Franklin raised one eyebrow. "They talk funny in Maine?"

Aurelia's cheeks turned pink in the dull glow of the lightbulb overhead. "Do you want me to feed Sassy, or do you want to make another attempt?"

Gavin took the bucket from her. "I'll feed the mare."

With a grimace, Aurelia stood back. "Are you sure you don't want me to? She's pretty skittish. But we can test the theory about her being afraid of males."

Sliding the stall door to the side, Gavin stood outside the stall, looking in at the horse.

Already, the whites of her eyes grew more disturbed. Sassy tossed her head and pawed at the ground.

Aurelia shook her head and reached for the bucket. "Please, let me. She's obviously upset." She took the bucket from Gavin. "Step back behind the door so she doesn't see you."

Gavin did as asked, peering over the top of the stall and gauging Sassy's reaction to the woman advancing into her stall. He'd be ready if the horse decided Aurelia was a threat.

As soon as Gavin stepped out of Sassy's line of sight, the mare settled onto all four hooves and reached out her nose, sniffing for the bucket of sweet feed.

"I'll be damned," Gavin muttered. "She really is afraid of men."

"That bastard who whipped her should get the whip for doing that," Young said.

"Agreed," Gavin whispered.

Aurelia hooked the bucket of feed on the wall and stepped back, aware of the mare at all times.

Sassy stayed back for a moment, her tail swishing.

Aurelia took another step away from the bucket.

Finally, Sassy moved forward and snuffled at the sweet feed. She eyed Aurelia for a second longer, and then stuck her nose in the bucket and munched on the grain.

Aurelia chuckled softly. "You're going to be all right." She reached out and patted the horse's neck.

Sassy pulled her head out of the bucket and leaned her cheek against Aurelia's face.

Scratching the animal's neck once more, Aurelia backed out of the stall and closed the door behind her, a smile curving her lips.

"You look like the cat that ate the cream," Gavin said.

"She's going to be all right." Her smile faded, and she glanced at Vasquez. "Are you okay?"

He gave her a crooked grin. "The only thing hurt on me is my head and my pride." He tipped his chin toward Sassy's stall. "How did you do that?"

"I think a lot had to do with me being a woman. Sassy didn't see any threat in me. Whereas, you're a man. A man hurt her, therefore, she thinks all men will hurt her. Time and patience will get her past her distrust of males."

"Well, I'm impressed," Young said. "We have a genuine horse whisperer among us. I don't suppose you could train a horse to muck its own stall, now, could you?" He winked.

Aurelia laughed. "Doubt it."

"Where did you learn how to work with horses?" Vasquez asked. "I didn't know one end of a horse from another before coming to Brighter Days."

Aurelia shrugged. "My parents made sure I had riding lessons. I spent more time in the stables than indoors. I guess you could say, I didn't have to be anyone but myself around the horses."

"And you had to be someone different around people?" Gavin asked.

"Sometimes..." She shrugged noncommittally. "Don't we all?"

Gavin sensed there was more to her story than she cared to share. He'd give her the time and space to learn to trust him with the whole truth. Until then, he'd have to be satisfied that she hadn't lied about knowing her way around horses. She was amazing. Any woman who could do what she'd just done was a woman after his own heart. One more reason to fall in love with her.

Love?

Gavin hadn't gone into this deal with unrealistic expectations. He didn't have to love the woman he married. At best, he'd hoped to like and respect her. He wanted a life partner and children he could love unconditionally. The thought of falling in love... excited and scared him at the same time. What if he fell in love with Aurelia, and she didn't love him in return? Did it matter? As long as he had a partner and children, did he care?

When he'd set out on this venture, he hadn't thought he'd care.

If he was truthful with himself, now, he knew it mattered. He just hoped it didn't matter too much. He didn't want to scare Aurelia away. He was just beginning to know her. And the more he knew, the more he liked.

Though, he could sense there were things she wasn't telling him. Hopefully soon, she'd feel comfortable enough to fill in all the blanks the application had left unclear.

CHAPTER 8

Aurelia brushed Sassy and spent time with her, letting her know she wouldn't hurt her. When she left the stall, Sassy nickered as if she was thanking her for her patience and understanding. Aurelia would bring the mare a treat the next day and spend more time with her, until the mare settled into her new life.

Assuming Aurelia would be around that long.

Not even a day had passed since she'd arrived at Brighter Days Rehabilitation Ranch, but she felt like it had been a lot longer. Her body was tired, though her mind was whizzing ahead, calculating the number of days she had left to fulfil the requirement of marriage and a baby before her thirtieth birthday. She had no guarantee that she'd get pregnant on her first try, even if she convinced Gavin to marry her within the next two weeks, she barely had time after that to make a baby. Suddenly, the narrow window of opportunity she had to work with seemed impossible and overwhelming.

And if she didn't get pregnant within the time she needed, and the reign of her country slipped into the hands of her odious second cousin Rupert, then what? She could be married to Gavin by then, anyway.

The thought of leaving her country behind and forging a path in Montana with Gavin held a great deal of appeal. She would just be Aurelia Blackstock, the bride of a military war hero. She would learn to share the responsibilities of cooking, help to build a house and raise children with a good man who deserved a lot better than to be tricked into marriage to serve as a stud to save the country.

While she'd spent time in the stall with Sassy, Aurelia could sense the presence of Gavin, looking out for her in case the mare spooked again. He shoveled fresh straw into the stall next to Sassy's and stacked bales of hay for ease of feeding the next day.

When Aurelia emerged, Gavin was there.

"I imagine you must be tired after traveling all day."

She nodded. "I am." Aurelia opened her mouth, wanting to confess all.

He took her hand in his and squeezed it gently as they walked toward the sprawling ranch house. "I want to apologize for my actions earlier. I shouldn't have accused you of wanting to hurt the people here at Brighter Days. I should have trusted you."

Her heart sank into her gut. Guilt twisted the knot there. "Gavin, you should know—"

He touched a finger to her lips. "What I know so far is that you're amazing and courageous. Not every woman would walk up to a spooked horse that easily weighs twenty times more than you. You could have been crushed."

She laughed. "Which makes me sound like an idiot for trying."

"No, you went with your gut. And your gut said the horse needed the benefit of a doubt, gentle care and a patient hand." He plucked a straw from her hair. "You gave her that. I should give you no less."

"You have the right to be suspicious," Aurelia started. "You don't know anything about me."

"I know what my gut tells me." He pulled her closer, the darkness settling around them.

"Hey, you two going to watch the news tonight?" Lori hurried past them in her gangly limp.

"We'll be there in a minute." Gavin started to pull Aurelia close again.

"The television in the bunkhouse isn't working," Franklin said from behind Gavin and Aurelia. He and Vasquez hurried past, pushing the wheelbarrow containing Young.

"We're going to make popcorn, watch the news

and then put a movie on. Want to join us?" Young said, holding onto the edges of the wheelbarrow.

Gavin stepped back from Aurelia. "I guess, we will."

Collin followed the younger guys.

Percy brought up the rear. "Might as well give it up. There's no privacy in a place like this."

"You got that right," Gavin muttered. He leaned close to Aurelia. "We'll talk tomorrow. I know a place where we won't be disturbed."

Aurelia nodded. Then she could tell him everything. About her life in Lastovia, about the need to marry and produce an heir. About why she really came to Montana. Then he was right to be suspicious and ask her to leave.

Hand in hand with Gavin, Aurelia walked to the house. She didn't want this to end. Not when she was just getting to know this man. And she liked him. A lot.

Inside, the pop, pop, pop of popcorn exploding inside the microwave and the sound of laughter echoed inside. The warm, buttery scent filled the air.

Gavin and Aurelia passed through the kitchen into the living room where everyone had congregated around the television.

"Want a beer?" Percy held out a long neck bottle toward Aurelia.

She hadn't had a beer since she'd attended a festival in her second year at college with Lilianna and other girls from her dorm. Aurelia nodded. "Please." She took the bottle from Percy and tipped it up. Cool liquid spilled down her throat and cooled her inside. "Mmm, that's good."

Percy handed Gavin the one in his other hand.

"I can get my own," Gavin said.

"Why, when you can have this one?" Percy pressed the beer into his hand. "Anyone else want a beer with your popcorn?"

Franklin and Young held up a hand.

"I'll take one," Taz said from his seat in a large leather lounge chair with Hannah sitting in his lap.

"What about you, Hannah?" Percy asked.

"I'll pass." She held up a glass. "Sticking to lemonade."

"Any reason why you're sticking to lemonade?" Percy's eyes narrowed. "Anything you want to share with the rest of us?"

Hannah's eyes widened innocently. "Nope."

"Oh, go ahead and tell them," Taz nuzzled her neck.

"Fine," she said. "I missed my period." She held up her hand. "I know, too much information, but I might be pregnant. I won't know until we get one of those home pregnancy tests."

"What?" Lori exploded. "You don't know, and you're not racing to Eagle Rock to find a kit? Are you insane?" She jumped up from her seat on the couch between Young and Vasquez. "I'll go."

"Sit down." Hannah grinned and waved at Lori. "It'll wait until tomorrow. Besides, I'm pretty sure I am." She stared at the beer Percy handed Taz. "Even the thought of beer makes me want to throw up." She covered her mouth. "And I missed two periods, not just one."

"Sweet Jesus, woman." Lori fell back on the couch. "I'd be a nervous wreck."

"Why?" Hannah asked. "Either I am or I'm not." She caught Taz's cheeks between her palms and kissed him soundly on the lips. "Either way, we're getting married." She held up her hand, brandishing the diamond ring on her left ring finger.

Lori popped up from the couch again and ran to hug Hannah.

Congratulations, hugging and handshaking were in order, and it took several minutes before the room quieted.

Aurelia hugged Hannah. "I'm very happy for you and Taz. You two look so happy together."

"Thank you. We are. I can't imagine what we'll do with a little one running around here. We're all so busy with the animals and guests."

"Franklin and I will help babysit," Vasquez said.

"Speak for yourself," Franklin said. "What do we know about babies?"

"I helped raise my baby sister. There's not much to it. You feed them and change diapers. They're eating, pooping machines for the first year of their lives." Vasquez winked at Hannah. "We'll help. I'll show Franklin the ropes."

Gavin hugged Hannah. "You're glowing, woman." He smiled down at her, holding her longer than the others.

Aurelia could see the special bond between Gavin and Hannah. Not a lover's bond, but one of very close friends, who were as close as brother and sister.

Her heart hurt as she remembered the bond she'd shared with her brother William. She missed her parents so much, it was like a raw wound in her heart.

"I've never been happier." Hannah straightened and reached out to hold Taz's hand. "Now, if you all are quite done, let's watch the news so we can get on with our movie." Hannah settled back in her seat on her fiancé's lap and adjusted the sound with the remote control.

The news came on, reporting information about a local rodeo coming to Bozeman and the status of the stock market after one of the major automakers announced a layoff.

"And in world news," the news anchor said, "the tiny European country of Lastovia is in an uproar."

Aurelia tensed. "Anyone need another beer?" she called out, her voice strained.

"I'll take one," Cookie said.

Aurelia turned away and started for the kitchen as the news anchor continued.

"Princess Olivia, the next royal in line to inherit the throne has disappeared." She cast a glance over her shoulder at the screen and cringed. A video of her greeting foreign dignitaries outside the Lastovia grand palace appeared on the monitor. She prayed the picture was too small and blurred for the group gathered around the television to recognize her.

"A world-wide hunt is underway to locate the missing princess," the reporter said. "The government of Lastovia is offering a two-hundred-and-fifty-thousand-dollar reward for information on her whereabouts. Foul play is suspected. It is believed the princess has been kidnapped."

"I'd like to collect that reward," Young said.

"What would you do with that kind of money?" Franklin asked.

"Buy a car," Young said.

Aurelia left the group watching the television and retreated to the kitchen where she found the beer in the refrigerator. By the time she returned to the living room, the news anchor had moved on to a story about the homeless problem in Seattle and then broke for a commercial.

Breathing a sigh, Aurelia handed the beer to Cookie.

"Thank you." He twisted the cap off the bottle and tipped the bottle up.

"You know," Young said. "That missing princess

looks familiar." He tapped a finger to his chin, squinting. "I just can't put my finger on it."

"I didn't get a close enough look at her," Franklin held out his hand. "Hand me that remote, so I can back it up and get a closer look. I could use two hundred and fifty thousand dollars to set up a gym back home in San Antonio."

Aurelia held her breath, praying they didn't reverse to the story about the missing princess.

Hannah held the remote tightly in her hand. "I want to get to the weather. We might need to cut the hay early if we have a lot of rain in the forecast."

Franklin, Vasquez and Young groaned as one.

"What?" Hannah shot a questioning look at them. "A little hard work going to kill you?"

"No, ma'am," Vasquez said, muttering something about itching and sweat beneath his breath.

The commercial ended and the weather came on. As Hannah suspected, rain was imminent in the forecast for the following week. "We need to cut the hay tomorrow and let it dry for a couple days before we can bale." She turned to Percy. "Do you think the rain will hold off for the hay to dry enough to bale by the end of this week?"

Percy nodded. "It's supposed to be dry and clear. As long as we get it cut tomorrow, we should be all right to bale before next weekend. I'll get the tractors ready in the morning."

"You and I will do the cutting."

"Should you be out there on a tractor all day," Taz asked.

"If I'm pregnant, riding on a tractor won't hurt me or the baby." She leaned in and kissed him. "But you can bring me water if you want to come check on me."

"I'll be on a job tomorrow."

"A job?" Hannah's eyebrows rose. "Hank have someone interesting for you to protect?"

Taz shrugged. "Some movie mogul coming out for a little R&R on Lena Love's ranch."

"Lena Love?" Aurelia's eyes widened. "The movie star?" Even in Lastovia, they watched many of the American movies.

Taz's lips twisted. "The one and only. Thankfully, she's on a shoot down in the Cayman Islands. One of the Brotherhood Protectors, Duke Morrison, is with her and her stunt double Angel Carson. Lena offered her place up for a mini-retreat for the director. Angel thinks she only did it in hopes the director will cast her in his next blockbuster."

"What is this Brotherhood Protectors?" Aurelia asked.

"A bunch of former military special operations guys who are working for Hank Patterson's security service, the Brotherhood Protectors." Taz grinned. "We serve as anything that's needed, from body-guards to undercover agents."

"Sounds interesting and potentially dangerous."

Aurelia liked the idea of highly trained military men providing security to others. She cast a glance in Collin's direction. Her bodyguard had similar qualifications, and she'd been lucky to find him.

"Hank's been trying to get Blackstock to join the brotherhood," Taz said. "Maybe you can talk him into it. As you know, he's a Navy SEAL. The best of the best. At least, they like to think they are." Taz winked.

Aurelia glanced at Gavin. "Why haven't you gone to work for Hank?"

"I like it here," he said, his voice low and tight. His fists clenched at his side.

Aurelia guessed Gavin was hesitant due to his missing leg. She also suspected he'd loved being a Navy SEAL and missed the excitement and challenge. A man didn't go through that kind of training to be satisfied with the slower pace of ranching.

The news ended, and Hannah put a video in the player. Percy dimmed the living room lights, and the crew settled in for the show.

After the first fifteen minutes of the movie, Aurelia found herself yawning. She leaned close to Gavin. "I'm going to get some air, and then go to bed."

"I'll come with you," he said.

"No, I won't be long. I'm just going to step outside for a moment, and then go straight upstairs." She touched his arm. "I could use some time alone. You enjoy the movie."

Gavin frowned. "You're not going out to check on the mare, are you?"

"No. I'm going out on the porch to stare at the stars for a moment. I don't think I've ever seen this many back home." When he started to go with her, she shook her head. "I won't be outside long."

He nodded. "I get it. Alone."

She gave him a brief smile, gathered some of the empty bottles and carried them into the kitchen where she set them on the counter. So much happened that day that she was feeling a little overwhelmed. And seeing the news about her disappearance made her question her decision to leave Lastovia. She stepped out on the deck, a million thoughts rushing through her head.

She hated to think of people wasting time looking for her, thinking something nefarious had happened to her. A part of her wanted to place a call to the Prime Minister and let him know she was okay but would be out of touch for the next ten months. But that would defeat the purpose of her getting away.

"Worried about home?" a voice said in the darkness.

She spun to face Collin, her heart in her throat as she looked around him. Had Gavin followed him outside?

"It's okay. Blackstock is still inside with the others."

Aurelia clasped her hands together, her gaze on the door, not Collin. "We shouldn't be talking."

"I just want to make sure you aren't going to bolt for home," Collin said. "And if you do, you'll let me know before you jump ship."

"I'm not going home." She straightened, lifting her chin. "I came here for a reason, and that reason still stands."

"I don't like that I can't be close enough to do my job," Collin said, his brow furrowing. "I heard you could have been killed by a horse today, while I was out mending a fence with Percy."

"I wasn't even close to being in danger." Aurelia smiled. "Besides, I'm surrounded by former military men who can protect me just as well."

Collin's frown deepened. "But that's my job."

"No, while you're here, you're a ranch hand. If trouble shows up, then I'll need you to resume your bodyguard duties. And right now, we're running the risk of being discovered."

He nodded. "I'm headed to the bunkhouse. You know where I am if you need me."

A noise at the door caught her attention, and she stiffened. "I'm fine out here on my own. But thank you for checking on me," she said for the benefit of anyone who might be standing inside the house, looking out from the shadows.

Collin gave her a mock salute and left the porch, headed for the bunkhouse.

Aurelia turned toward the Montana sky and lifted her face to the stars. Oh, to be unencumbered of royal obligations. To be free to make decisions that only impacted herself, not tens of thousands of her subjects. If she failed to meet the deadline, she could be free to pursue life as she saw fit. She didn't have to stay in Lastovia. She would be free to travel the world as she'd originally intended before her parents and brother had died in the car crash.

The thought of Rupert, her second cousin, taking the reign turned her stomach. The man was greedy and would milk the government for every penny he could wring out of the coffers. And he would not be a good diplomat to represent their gentle country at international summits. He would destroy all the good will Aurelia's parents had worked so hard to generate during their reign.

She stiffened her resolve as she stiffened her spine. For her country, she would follow through on her plan to wed and breed. It was the least she could do to protect her country. If it meant dropping out of sight for a few months, so be it. She knew she would return as soon as she had succeeded at her plan.

Hopefully, Gavin wouldn't back out when he discovered she was a princess looking for a stud service to protect her legacy. Looking back, she realized the news report tonight could have served as the opening she needed to inform Gavin of her real identity and her reason for being in Montana, anxiously needing to be a bride. Yes, she wanted children and a husband. Both were requisite of the title. But once she had both, would it be as easy to leave Montana as it had been getting there?

Would Gavin follow her back to Lastovia? Or would he refuse to leave Montana, his home? She wouldn't blame him if he didn't want to go with her. But she didn't want to leave without him. Children needed their father. Surely, he'd care enough to come with her and their child.

By all that was holy, her plan was a lot more complicated than she'd ever thought. Especially when emotions were involved.

CHAPTER 9

GAVIN STEPPED BACK into the shadows by the door. He hadn't intended to spy on Aurelia, but he'd worried she'd go back out to the barn and check on Sassy without backup. If the horse spooked and hurt Aurelia, no one would know, and she could lie there in the dark until morning.

But that's not where she'd gone.

He'd seen Collin leave the living room, but he hadn't expected him to be outside on the porch, chatting with Aurelia. They'd appeared to be in an intense discussion but had talked so softly, Gavin hadn't caught their words, only a few.

Collin seemed concerned that Aurelia had almost been killed by a horse. When Aurelia assured him that there were others there to protect her, he'd said something about it being his job.

What had he meant? His job to protect her...?

For that matter, it had been pretty coincidental that he'd shown up on the same bus as Aurelia.

During all his years as a Navy SEAL, Gavin had been convinced there was no such thing as coincidence. Why had he accepted the Collin-Aurelia synchronized arrival?

From what he could tell, Collin knew Aurelia, as more than just a passing acquaintance on public transportation. Why would they hide that from him and from the others at Brighter Days? They hadn't touched, kissed or held hands. He didn't get the impression they were anything closer than friends, but it still begged the question, why didn't they want anyone to know they knew each other?

He waited a few minutes before he finally pushed through the door and out onto the porch.

Aurelia leaned against a post, staring out at the brilliantly lit sky filled with glittering stars.

"Sorry, I thought you'd be upstairs by now," Gavin lied.

"I thought I would be, too, but I couldn't tear myself away from the view of the starlight reflected off the snow-capped peaks." She sighed. "It's amazing."

"The skies are so clear you feel like you can see to the next galaxy," Gavin said.

"Exactly," she said, her voice little more than a whisper, as if she stood in a library, afraid to disturb the peace and quiet.

For a long moment, Gavin held his tongue. He couldn't ask her what Collin meant to her without revealing he'd overheard them talking. That would mean admitting he'd been spying on her. It would demonstrate his lack of faith and trust in her. He might not ask the questions, but he'd be more observant where the two of them were concerned. She'd come to Montana under the pretext of marrying him as a mail-order bride. Why would she bring Collin along if she was set to marry another man?

"Aurelia?"

"Yes?" She turned to face him.

"Why did you come to Montana?" Gavin asked.

She frowned. "You know why I came. I want to marry and have children. I don't want to wait until my eggs dry up and I'm incapable of bearing children of my own."

"You put a lot of faith in a stranger. I could have been a real horse's ass and abusive."

She smiled. "But you're not." Aurelia cupped his cheek and tilted her head up to stare into his face. Starlight glinted off her eyes, making them sparkle. "And you gave me the chance to back out if I didn't think we would be compatible."

"And now? Why are you staying?" he asked, still holding back, not reaching out when he ached to do so.

"Now..." Her smile faded as she stared into his eyes. "I'm more convinced than ever...I made the right decision." Her brow dipped. "Why do you ask?" Her frown deepened. "Are you having second thoughts?"

He didn't answer right away.

Aurelia's eyes widened. "You are." She shook her head. "I know I can be stubborn, and sometimes headstrong, but I don't ever do anything out of spite. I can work hard, if you show me what you need done." She rested her hands on his chest. "I think this can work. I really do. Just give me a chance."

Oh, hell. Who was he kidding? The woman might not be telling him the entire truth, but he couldn't stop what was happening. Not when she looked at him with stars in her eyes. When she touched him and leaned her body against his, his brain scrambled. She could be a serial killer, and he'd go willingly to the slaughter.

Gavin gathered her in his arms. "I don't know what to believe or who to trust, but I know one thing…" He dipped his head, his lips brushing across hers briefly. "I can't resist you. I feel like a moth to your flame."

"And you're afraid you'll get burned." She touched her lips to his. "The last thing I want is for you to be hurt." She leaned up and pressed her lips harder to his.

Gavin crushed her in his arms, his mouth coming down on hers, his tongue pushing past her teeth to sweep across hers, staking his claim. This woman had come to him. To be his partner, his wife. He wanted her. Anything else seemed to fade by the wayside as he kissed Aurelia.

When he at last raised his head, he stared down into her eyes. "I want you to know...I don't like to share."

Her lips quirked upward. "That sentiment goes both ways. Neither do I."

If she was going to tell him what was going on between her and Collin, his statement would have been a good lead-in. Apparently, she wasn't going to fill him in on her relationship with the ranch hand.

Gavin brushed his thumb across her lips. "We have a long way to go getting to know and trust each other."

She nodded. "We'll work on that. There's so much I want to know about you and want you to know about me."

"I guess we'll take it one day at a time." He pulled her into his arms and just held her.

Aurelia wrapped her arms around his waist and leaned into him.

He liked the way she felt against him. Her soft curves and sweet scent reminded him of all he'd missed since he'd been injured. All he'd denied himself, thinking he wouldn't find a woman who would accept him for who and what he was. He still didn't know how she would react when she saw what was left of his leg when he wasn't wearing the prosthetic. As much as she said it didn't matter to her, she might not be able to handle the reality.

"Are you sure you want to go forward with our plan?"

She nodded. "I'm still on board. And, like I said, I'm not getting any younger. I don't want to miss the opportunity to have a family...children of my own." She leaned her cheek against his chest. "I came here with the intention of marrying you. I haven't changed my mind."

He chuckled. "Why? I'm not rich. I barely have enough money for a down payment on my own home. But I work hard, and I'll protect my family with everything I've got. I might not be the best choice for a husband, but I'm loyal, and you can trust me to be there for you and always tell you the truth." He paused. "Unless of course, you ask me how you look in certain outfits. I'm not a fashion critic. And I'm sure anything you wear will be gorgeous."

Aurelia laughed. "You don't have to convince me. I pride myself in my ability to know and understand different people. I knew from your blunt ad you were a straight-talking man of integrity."

"You got that from my ad?" He shook his head. "I can't lie. Lori wrote the ad. The whole mail-order bride thing was her idea."

She smiled. "I had that feeling when Lori told me she knew. She's a good friend, and she's looking out for you."

Gavin could have stood there all night with his cheek pressed against Aurelia's hair and his arms wrapped around her. But other parts of him were getting more excited by the moment. Was it too soon to take it to the next level?'

Sadly, yes. He didn't want to scare her away yet. When they made love, he wanted her to want it as badly as he did.

He set her away from him. "I'd better call it a night before I forget I'm trying to build your trust."

She nodded. "We have tomorrow to get to know each other better."

"And the next day."

Her smile stretched across her face, looking a little wistful.

He couldn't resist adding, "Before you know it, we'll have the rest of our lives."

"If things progress the way they are..." Aurelia finished. "Goodnight, Gavin."

"Goodnight, Aurelia. I'm really glad we met."

"Me, too." She pushed up on her toes and gave him a quick peck on the lips. Then she ran into the house.

Which was just as well. Had she stood there another second, he wouldn't have been able to walk away. He'd have pulled her into his arms again. And then he might not have had the willpower to wait for the right moment to make love to her.

. . .

Aurelia ran all the way up the stairs to the top and into her room before she slowed and took a breath.

Sweet heaven, she had wanted to stay in Gavin's arms all night long. He was so strong, the muscles in his chest so hard, they could have been a stone wall. And when he'd wrapped his arms around her, she'd melted into him, wishing she could stay there forever.

Every time she was near him reinforced her decision to come to Montana. Being here was the right thing. Marrying Gavin was the best idea. Ever.

One day at a time. That's how they would build on their relationship.

But she didn't have a lot of time to reach the proper conclusion.

Aurelia fished her toiletries kit out of her suitcase and crossed the hall to the bath room. She brushed her teeth, washed her face and pulled her hair up into a knot at the crown of her head before securing it with a ponytail elastic.

When she was done, she looked to be about fourteen years old.

She didn't care. After the danger and sleepless hours of getting to Montana, she was ready to sleep. Tomorrow, she needed to be at her best to work on making Gavin fall in love with her. She hadn't realized just how much she wanted this until they'd kissed.

When she opened the door to the bathroom and

peeked out, the hallway was clear, and Gavin's bedroom door was open, the light off inside. Apparently, he was either downstairs or still outside. That would give her a little time to place a call back home to Lilianna. She'd promised to let her friend know she'd made it okay and everything was all right.

Aurelia hurried back across the hall and into her room. She closed the door and dug out the burner phone she'd purchased upon entry into the US. She'd read up on the internet and learned that WIFI and cell phone service in rural Montana was sketchy at best. She held the disposable phone in front of her and checked for a signal, surprised there actually was one. Aurelia walked into the closet on the side of the room away from Gavin's and closed the door.

She entered Lilianna's phone number, pressed the talk button and held the phone up to her ear, her heart pounding. She'd called Lilianna before when she'd made it to the US. With the news report on her country's frantic search for their princess, Aurelia couldn't help but feel sad that her country was worried about her. If she'd had any other choice, she wouldn't have left. But to protect any man she considered marrying, and herself, she'd had to go into hiding.

"Hello?" a sleepy voice said on the other side of the world.

Aurelia held the phone tightly in her hand, a wave

of homesickness washing over her at the sound of her friend's voice. "Hey, Lili, it's me."

"Oh, dear, sweet Jesus." The sleepiness vanished out of Lilianna's voice. "How are you? Did you get there all right? Is he as dreamy as his picture? I miss you so much."

Aurelia laughed. "I'm okay. I'm here at the Brighter Days Rehabilitation Ranch in the room next to him."

"And?" Lilianna prompted.

"He's even dreamier than his photo," Aurelia admitted, her pulse fluttering at the remembered kisses.

"Have you told him who you are?"

"Not yet. I want him to get to know me before all that gets in the way."

"Do you like him?" Lilianna asked. "You still have time to back out of anything more permanent. Just you remember that. You're not obligated to marry him."

"I know. I imagined it would be no big deal to marry someone I just met, but it's not as easy as I thought it would be."

"Is he a jerk? Because, if he is, I'll be there on the next flight out of Lastovia. I shouldn't have let you go. This idea was beyond crazy."

Aurelia smiled at the phone. "No, Lili, he's actually quite wonderful. It's me. I haven't told him why I want to marry and have children. I feel like the jerk, here." Her shoulders slumped. "And if anyone learns where I am, it puts Gavin in danger. I haven't been fair to him. And he's a fine man who believes in truth, trust and loyalty. I'm not sure how he'll react when he finds out about me and my...obligations." Her voice caught. "Lili, what if he doesn't want to come to Lastovia? And worse...what if he doesn't want our child to leave the US?"

"Hmmm." For a long moment, that was the only sound Lilianna made. "You are in a pickle."

"I want him to get to know me first. If we can't make a go of being a couple, none of this will mean a thing. A marriage wouldn't last if we can't stand each other."

"I take it that's not an issue on your part," Lilianna drawled.

"No," Aurelia admitted. "I like him. A lot."

"Oh, Aurie, if you like him, this will work. You're one of the most likable princesses I've ever met."

Aurelia laughed. "I'm the only princess you've ever met."

"True," Lilianna said. "The point is that he's bound to fall in love with you, if he hasn't already."

"I hope so," she said, and meant it. "But will he forgive me for keeping the truth from him?"

"He has to. Because he has to love you." Lilianna sighed. "Aurie, what's not to love?"

"My lies. That's what's not to love." She drew in a deep breath and let it out slowly, willing the tension to release from her shoulders. She was so tired from the journey, the intrigue and from the carrying the weight of her subterfuge. "I'd better go before someone hears me. I'm sitting in a closet to keep that from happening."

Lilianna snickered. "I can just picture that. The princess of Lastovia, sitting in a dark, tiny closet while her country is frantically searching for her."

"About that...is everything okay, otherwise?" Aurelia felt the tension seep back into her neck and shoulders.

"We haven't fallen apart yet, but your cousin Rupert is posturing to be your replacement. I wouldn't stay 'missing' for too long."

"Understood. As soon as I can, I'll let the world know I'm not dead or kidnapped. Until then, I need to get a man to fall in love with me, ask me to marry him and then give me the child I need to secure my reign. Piece of cake, as the Americans would say."

"You make me tired just thinking of it. I wish you well and happy. Be safe. I'll contact you if Rupert gets too comfortable sitting on your throne."

"Thank you, Lili," Aurelia said. "You're a good person and a good friend. I could not have done this without your help."

"That's what friends are for."

Aurelia rang off, warmed by the love she felt for her friend since primary school. She sat for a minute or two longer in the bottom of the closet, going over all that had happened that day. All in all, it had been a good day. She'd met the man she wanted to be her husband and the father of her children. He wasn't completely averse to the idea of her as his wife. Aurelia would consider that a huge win. She was truly lucky to have found such a fine man, who was willing to give her a chance to prove herself a suitable mate.

Exhaustion drained what little energy she had left. If she didn't get up and go to bed soon, she'd end up sleeping in the closet overnight.

Before she got to that level of need, she pushed to her feet, staggered into the bedroom, ripped off her clothes and rubbed lotion into her skin. Feeling a little better, she rummaged through her little suitcase for underclothing and a nightgown.

Once dressed for bed, she walked to the wall she shared with Gavin and listened for sounds of movement on the other side.

After a minute, she heard a chair scrape across the wooden floor and the sound of drawers opening and closing.

Her insides heated. She pressed a fist to her chest and imagined what Gavin might be wearing, or not wearing. Did he dress for bed or slide in naked?

The heat in her neck and face spread south to her core. Her exhaustion flew out the window as desire flooded her body.

If she didn't screw this up, a union between her

and the Navy SEAL would be incredibly satisfying. She had no doubt they'd be great together in bed. He'd more than make up for the fact he had only one leg. She had a feeling it wouldn't slow him down one little bit.

Her breathing growing ragged, Aurelia tore herself away from the wall and climbed into the bed, pulling the blankets up to her chin. But sleep wouldn't come for another couple of hours. Her heart beat a rapid tattoo long into the night with each thought she had about the man in the room next door.

CHAPTER 10

GAVIN TOSSED and turned throughout the night. The fact Aurelia lay in a bed on the other side of a single wall kept him awake far into the wee hours of the morning. All the questions he wanted to ask churned in his brain until he gave up on sleep and stared up at the ceiling.

What was she hiding?

What was it between her and Collin?

What position did she like best when making love?

Oh, sweet Lord, he had to go there. Once on the path to mind sex, he couldn't deviate until he'd gone all the way.

Around two in the morning, he rose from the bed, slipped on a pair of shorts that tented in the front and crossed the hall to the bathroom. A long, cool shower helped but didn't completely alleviate his need.

He wanted Aurelia, whether he could trust her or not. He needed her like he needed to breathe, like his heart needed to beat. And he'd known her not even twenty-four hours. This was pure insanity. Love at first sight didn't exist.

However, *lust* at first sight was not only possible, but the likely conclusion he had to accept. He was in lust with the lovely stranger.

Gavin had to remind himself he wasn't an animal. A woman should be treated with respect. She should be wooed gently and carefully so as not to scare her away. God, he didn't want to scare Aurelia away. Now that she was there, he wanted to see if the connection he felt was equally experienced by her.

Tomorrow, he kept telling himself. He'd put into play his plan to court the pretty mail-order bride. Though she'd come to marry him, she had to know for certain that was what she wanted. He had to prove to her that he was worthy of her trust and loyalty.

With a plan in mind, he finally fell into a deep sleep, waking only when the sun knifed through the window and slashed across his eyelids. His eyes blinked open, and he shot a glance at the clock on the nightstand. Already seven, the rest of the residents of Brighter Days would be up and doing their pre-breakfast chores.

Gavin shot out of the bed, shoved his stump into the special sock and then the prosthetic leg, strapped it in place, and then slid into his blue jeans. Once again, he wondered how Aurelia would respond to seeing him naked. Hopefully, he'd know soon enough. Within the week, he wanted to test their compatibility in bed. Or was that too soon? Damn, he hadn't dated in so long he didn't know the rules. And what were the rules on easing a woman into a relationship with a man with a disability?

Hannah chose to think of it not as a *disability* but matter of different *abilities*. Whatever. He was different and hoped that didn't make Aurelia change her mind. He'd been up front in his advertisement... She'd known before she came... Still, Gavin's confidence in this one respect was lacking.

Well, he'd just have to get over it and prove to Aurelia that he could do anything any two-legged man could do. He could have been a lot worse off. He had two strong arms and one perfectly functioning leg. That was a lot more than many of the men had that he'd spent time with in physical therapy. More than Young had. And look at Young. The man had more spirit and chutzpah than most men with all four limbs intact.

Once he was fully dressed, Gavin left his room, slowing as he passed Aurelia's to listen for sounds of movement within. Silence. Not even a hint of whether she was still asleep or already out and about.

Gavin descended the steps to the ground floor and followed the clanging of pots and pans to the kitchen.

Cookie stood at the stove, frying bacon.

Next to him was Aurelia, stirring frothy, golden scrambled eggs in a skillet. She looked up with a warm, welcoming smile. "How's this for a first? I'm making scrambled eggs." With a grimace, she scraped the spatula across the bottom of the pan. "I hope I'm not burning them."

"These guys aren't picky, even if you do," Cookie said. "They'll eat anything that doesn't bite them first."

"True." Hannah crossed the kitchen carrying a pitcher of orange juice and a carton of milk. "The rest of the guys are out taking care of the animals. You can man the toaster and keep it going."

Gavin nodded, glad to help in the kitchen for once. It gave him the opportunity to be closer to Aurelia and prove to her that he could be just as helpful in the house as outside. A lot of men considered household chores a woman's work. Not Gavin. And not Cookie. Food nourished the body. People couldn't perform the work that needed done without a hearty meal. Having been a bachelor most of his life, Gavin knew his way around a kitchen. He found it strange that, at nearly thirty years old, Aurelia had never learned to cook. What did she do for meals? Eat out all the time?

He added that to the list of questions he intended to get answers for. Soon.

Lori entered through the back door, her face flushed with the cool morning air. "Good morning!"

"Good morning, Lori," Aurelia said with a smile.

"Breakfast is almost ready," Hannah said. "Are the guys coming?"

"Yes, ma'am. They're washing up outside. I chose to come inside to do the same. By the way, Lucky's doing great. He's finally caught up to the size of the other puppies." Lori hurried through the kitchen and down the hallway to the bathroom.

Aurelia scraped the scrambled eggs from the pan onto a platter Cookie had placed on the counter beside the stove. She carried the platter to the table and came back to help Gavin butter the toast.

By the time they had a nice neat stack ready, the others were filing into the kitchen, laughing and joking with each other.

Collin and Percy were last to arrive, behind the younger men.

"Where's Taz?" Percy asked.

Hannah's lips twisted. "He got a call from Hank. He's not going to work the Love ranch. Instead he'll be on assignment in Bozeman for the next couple days."

"Good thing the weather's holding off. We won't need to haul hay now for another couple of weeks," Percy said. "We're caught up with the chores if you want to make a trip into Bozeman for supplies today."

Hannah nodded. "I could use some groceries and cleaning supplies." She glanced at the others. "Anyone else want to head to Bozeman?"

"I could use some new gloves," Young said. "And I was thinking about getting a cowboy hat."

"Finally coming over to the dark side of ranch life?" Franklin said.

Young nodded. "I think it will make me look taller." He winked at Aurelia. "Girls love tall guys, right?"

Aurelia smiled.

"I think girls love guys who treat them with tender, loving care and a whole lot of respect," Hannah said. "Doesn't matter if they're short or tall."

"Still, I want to check out the western store and get a hat." Young grinned. "I'm in for a ride to Bozeman."

The men gathered around the table and waited for the women to be seated before they settled.

"What about the rest of you?" Hannah asked as she passed the scrambled eggs to her right.

"I'm cleaning the refrigerator," Lori said. "It's past due, and I promised Cookie I'd help reorganize the cabinets and pantry."

Cookie held up a hand. "I'm with Lori today."

"Collin?" Hannah cast a glance at the new ranch hand.

"I have cleaning detail in the bunkhouse. I want to get it done before noon. Then I'm going to work out."

"Work out?" Franklin blinked. "Ranch life isn't enough?"

"It's good for arms and abs, but I'd like to get a good run in."

"If I'm done with the cabinets and refrigerator, I might join you," Lori said. "I promise not to slow you down too much. I know a fairly smooth route where you won't twist an ankle."

Gavin fought a grin. Lori could run circles around most two-legged people.

Collin gave her a chin lift. "You're on."

Vasquez shoveled eggs onto his plate and passed them on. "Sounds like too much work for me. Franklin and I are going to work on the stairs that lead up into the hayloft. Some of the boards are dry-rotted through."

Hannah smiled and handed Aurelia the pitcher of orange juice. "Do you want to go to Bozeman with us, Aurelia?"

She shook her head. "I'm looking forward to not being in a vehicle. I want to enjoy some of the clean, mountain air Montana is famous for."

"And I'm going to show her around the ranch, if she'll let me," Gavin said, his gaze capturing Aurelia's.

She smiled. "I'd like that."

"On horseback?" he asked.

Her smile broadened. "Even better."

Breakfast was over not long after. Everyone helped clear the table and stack the dishes in the sink.

"Cookie and I will finish the kitchen cleanup. You guys go on," Lori said. When Gavin walked by, she snagged his arm. "Except you. I think you need to take a picnic lunch. I'll put some sandwiches together, along with something to drink."

"Thanks, Lori. That's what I had in mind."

Aurelia had left the kitchen to go up to change into boots and a light jacket.

Lori pulled the roast from two nights before out of the refrigerator and cut slices off, laying them on a plate. "You need to take Aurelia up to the waterfall."

"Again, that's what I had in mind." Gavin shook his head. "You'd think I didn't know how to treat a lady."

Lori slapped four slices of bread on the plate and layered them with the roast beef. "Well, it's been a while, am I right? Mustard or mayo?"

"Yes, it has and mustard."

"Are you sure that's what Aurelia would want?"

"One of each," Gavin acquiesced. "That way she can choose."

Lori gave him a tight smile. "That's better. Be a gentleman. Help her down from her horse. Don't come on too strong." She dropped her voice to a whisper. "And for all that's holy, don't push the sex."

Gavin burst out laughing. "You're giving me

advice?" He raised an eyebrow. "How long has it been since you've been out on a date?"

Her eyes narrowed. "None of your business." She poked a finger at his chest. "Don't screw this up. I like Aurelia. She'd be good for you."

He gave her a mock salute. "Yes, ma'am."

"And don't ma'am me. I wasn't an officer. I worked for a living." She wrapped the sandwiches in plastic wrap and pulled two bottles of water from the refrigerator. "Do your best. I know you're a good guy. But you have to show her that you are." She shoved the food and drinks into his hands and gave him a hug. "Go get her."

"Go get who?" Cookie asked.

"No one," Lori sang. "Let's get this kitchen cleaned up."

Gavin carried the sandwiches and water bottles out to the barn and stashed them in a saddlebag. He brought Ranger, his favorite bay gelding out of the stall and tied him to a post. Then he led Misty, one of the gentlest mares on the ranch, out of her stall and tied her to the post next to Ranger. He'd saddled Ranger and was carrying a smaller saddle out for Misty when Aurelia entered the barn.

"Then we are riding today, as planned?" she asked.

He nodded. "I thought I could take you out on the ranch and show you what this place is all about."

"I would love that." She eyed the small mare

standing docilely beside his gelding. "Is this the horse you've chosen for me?"

"This is Misty. She's about the sweetest-tempered mare you'll find in the stable."

Aurelia ran her hand along Misty's neck. "No offense, Misty, but I think I'd rather take Sassy out for some exercise."

"No way." Gavin still held the saddle in his arms. "Sassy isn't ready for anyone to ride her."

"I have a feeling Sassy has been highly misunderstood." Aurelia untied Misty from the post and led her back to her stall. "Sorry, darling, but not today."

With his hands full of a saddle, Gavin couldn't stop Aurelia from marching Misty back into her stall. "Don't you think you should start with a horse with a known personality?"

Aurelia didn't respond, but latched Misty's stall and walked to the last stall in the barn.

"Aurelia, that horse is dangerous. Please don't go—"

Gavin almost threw the saddle on the ground when the fool woman opened Sassy's stall and walked right in.

"Hey, you big, beautiful baby," Aurelia crooned to the mare as she led her out of her stall and tied her lead to a hook on a post. "I bet you just want to get outside and run like the wind."

"I don't know if this is a good idea," Gavin hedged.

Sassy danced sideways at the sound of Gavin's voice.

"It's okay," Aurelia said, her voice even and calming. "He's not going to hurt you. He's one of the good guys." She turned and took the saddle blanket from Gavin and held it under Sassy's nose. "Remember one of these?"

Sassy tossed her head as if to say yes. But she didn't go crazy or try to back away.

"That's right. It feels good on your back." Aurelia rubbed the blanket along Sassy's neck and up over her shoulders until it was lying across her back.

Gavin released the saddle into Aurelia's arms. "Even if you get the saddle on her, that doesn't mean she'll let you ride," he whispered.

"Sassy and I have an understanding," Aurelia said. "I won't hurt her, and she won't hurt me." She held the saddle beneath Sassy's nose and let her sniff, before she eased it along the animal's side.

Gavin wanted to take the saddle from Aurelia and toss it onto the mare's back. But he knew it would only spook Sassy.

The method Aurelia was using seemed to be working, so he stayed back, allowing Aurelia the autonomy to do what she thought best.

But that didn't keep Gavin from holding his breath as the mare pawed the ground.

And his heart stopped for a second when Sassy tried to back up, pulling hard on the lead.

Aurelia paused and talked to the mare again, her words silly, nonsensical and delivered in an even tone.

Sassy settled down, and Aurelia slid the saddle onto her back.

In the next few minutes, she had the girth tightened around the mare's belly and the stirrups adjusted.

Gavin couldn't believe this was the same horse that had almost killed Vasquez the day before.

But she still hadn't gotten the bridle on the mare. If a horse wanted to be stubborn, clamping its mouth closed was a good place to start.

Aurelia looked up. "Bridle?"

"In the tack room." He held up a hand. "I'll get it." He returned a moment later to find her using the brush to scratch behind Sassy's ears. The mare leaned into the brush, obviously enjoying the treatment.

Aurelia took the bridle from Gavin and approached the mare like she had with the blanket and saddle.

Sassy tossed her head and turned away.

Not to be deterred, Aurelia moved closer and held out her other hand with a piece of a carrot on her palm.

Sassy tossed her head again but came back to sniff at the carrot. She picked it out of Aurelia's hand with her soft lips.

After the horse chewed the carrot, Aurelia slipped

the bridle over her nose and settled the straps over her ears. "See? That wasn't so bad, was it?"

Sassy nodded her head.

Aurelia laughed and turned to Gavin. "We're ready, I think."

"I hope you're right. At the first sign of her going off the deep end, you're off and she's back in her stall. Deal?"

"First sign?" Aurelia rubbed Sassy's nose. "Everyone deserves a second chance."

"Not today." Gavin pressed his lips together and waited for Aurelia's agreement.

"Okay, first sign, I'll back off today." She smoothed her hand over the mare's neck. "But I'm not giving up on her. I feel like she's got a lot more to offer than her previous owner expected."

Gavin led his gelding out of the barn and waited for Aurelia and Sassy to follow. When they didn't come right out, he worried something might have happened. But then Aurelia led Sassy out of the barn as easily as if the horse was Misty, not a half-crazed, abused animal.

"You know you don't have to prove you know your way around horses, don't you?" Gavin said. "I'd rather know you're safe than right."

She shook her head. "I'm not trying to make a point with you. I'm more concerned about Sassy. It's as if I can feel her pain. I want her to know she's going to be better, now that she's at Brighter Days."

"I think she's well on her way to that goal. But you don't have to ride her today. Perhaps just getting a saddle on her was enough for one day."

Aurelia slid a hand along Sassy's neck. "I think she'll be okay with me on her back. Didn't they say she used to belong to a woman who rode her before she was sold to that odious man?"

"That's what Hannah said."

"I think she'll remember and behave." Aurelia brightened. "There's one way to find out." She turned toward the horse, slipped the reins along the side of the horse's neck, gripped the saddle horn and stuck her foot in the stirrup.

Sassy shifted nervously and whinnied.

Aurelia straightened in the stirrup and slung her leg over the mare's back.

Sassy spun in a circle before she settled down.

If Gavin had doubts about Aurelia's riding ability, they were eased when he saw how she sat with her back ramrod straight and her hands lightly holding the reins. The woman obviously knew how to ride. And nothing was sexier than a woman riding a horse. She had grace, strength and confidence in the way she carried herself in the saddle.

Gavin fit his good foot in the stirrup, flung his leg over the gelding's back and settled into the saddle. He had to lean over to fit his prosthetic foot into the other stirrup. He did it quickly and efficiently, not wanting to draw attention to himself or to his disability.

Once he was seated in the saddle and stirrups, he turned his horse toward the pasture gate, leaned over and unhooked the latch. He pushed the gate wide and rode Ranger through. On the other side, he stopped and waited for Aurelia and Sassy. He prayed the mare wouldn't balk passing through the gate.

Aurelia spoke to the horse, leaning over her neck to whisper into the animal's ear. She nudged Sassy's flanks with her heels and the mare leaped through the gate, shot past Gavin and Ranger and galloped across the pasture, with no indication she would slow until she crossed the border into the next state.

"Go! I'll close the gate," Percy called out, running toward the fence.

"Do you need help?" Collin called out, racing ahead of Percy.

"No. I'll catch her," Gavin yelled back as he urged Ranger to catch up to Sassy and her rider. Aurelia knew how to sit a horse, but Gavin prayed she knew how to *stay* on a runaway horse. Sassy could come across a fence, stop suddenly and throw Aurelia into the barbed wire.

Or worse, she could plow right into the fence and get horse and rider wrapped in barbed wire so badly, it could kill them both.

Scenario after scenario rolled through Gavin's mind like a high-speed movie reel that wouldn't quit.

He had to get to Aurelia before anything horrible happened

With the need to be in the lead as natural to Ranger as being male and randy, the gelding stretched out his legs and body and powered after the mare.

All of Gavin's worst fears seemed to be coming to fruition as Sassy made a beeline for a section of the fence covered in vines. She didn't slow at all as she approached.

Gavin cringed, certain the horse and rider would end up with terrible injuries.

Just as the mare reached the vine-covered fence, she bunched her back legs and leaped over the obstacle, sailing through the air as light as an African gazelle.

His heart pounding like a bass drum in a marching band Gavin watched as the horse and rider flew over the fence. Aurelia held on, leaning forward over Sassy's neck as the horse rose into the air. She pitched forward as the horse hit the ground on the other side. But she retained her seat in the saddle and came out of the jump with a huge smile on her face. "Did you see that?" she called out over her shoulder. "Did you see her fly?" Aurelia called out, her voice shaking with excitement.

Not only had he seen it, he'd suffered every second of it. And for nothing. Aurelia had handled the horse brilliantly, a natural in the saddle and so very beautiful.

Gavin finally remembered to breathe. He rode his horse to the gate that would lead into the pasture in which Sassy had jumped. He let himself through and guided his gelding toward the clump of horses standing at one end of a pasture. In the middle of the herd, Sassy stood with Aurelia on her back, her sides heaving with exertion.

When Gavin got close enough, he could see the smile on Aurelia's face. It nearly outshone the stars from last night. The sun shined down on Aurelia's beautiful blond hair, and her face was wreathed in a smile. Never mind she'd scared the beejeezus out of him. The horse and woman had both remained uninjured.

His lips pressed tightly together, Gavin shook his head. "Where in the hell did you learn to jump like that?"

CHAPTER 11

AURELIA COULDN'T LIE. She'd been terrified when Sassy headed straight for the fence. Though she'd tried to pull back on the reins, the horse had clamped the bit between her teeth and wasn't going to slow down. She'd charged the vine-covered fence as if she knew exactly what she was doing. When she'd left the ground, Aurelia had held on, her legs clamped tightly around the mare's sides. Her years in dressage and jumping had paid off when she hadn't flown out of the saddle and broken her neck.

Sassy had known exactly what she was doing and had cleared the fence with no problem whatsoever.

Once they'd landed, Sassy joined a herd of horses on the other side and relaxed enough to grab a mouthful of grass.

Thrilled to be alive, and happy to now know what

Sassy's original owner had trained her to do, Aurelia couldn't help smiling when Gavin joined her.

The stern look on his face did nothing to take away from the pure joy of being outdoors and riding like she'd done in her teens and early twenties. "It's a glorious day. Please don't be mad at me."

"I'm not mad," Gavin said. "Worried, but not mad." His frown deepened. "We're going up into the mountains. Do you think you can control the mare on narrow trails?"

Aurelia leaned over the mare's neck and patted her. "I think she had to get some energy out of her system. She seems to have calmed down."

"We'll play it by ear. If she starts acting up, we'll come back down."

"Fair enough." She sat up and grinned. "You lead, we'll follow."

Gavin led the way up a mountain trail. As the sun rose higher, the earth heated, making it warm enough Aurelia shed her jacket, tying it around her waist. The views between the trees were of rocky bluffs, evergreen trees and valleys full of lovely wildflowers.

After looking over his shoulder for the tenth time to make sure Sassy wasn't acting up, Gavin finally relaxed and trusted Aurelia would be okay.

Talking wasn't an option with them traveling single-file up the mountain trail, which also wasn't conducive to learning more about the stranger in front of her. Aurelia hoped he would stop soon, and they could get on with learning more about each other. After her conversation with Lilianna the night before, Aurelia was convinced she had to tell Gavin who she was and what they were up against should they continue to see each other and eventually marry. He needed to know he might be in danger, should whomever didn't want her to marry, finally catch up with her.

Thirty minutes later, Gavin entered a forest glen, crossed an open meadow and stopped short of a stand of trees.

"Are we stopping here?" Aurelia called out.

"We are." Gavin dropped down out of the saddle, hopping until he could get his legs steady.

He hurried toward Sassy, reaching out to assist Aurelia from her saddle.

She started to tell him not to bother but didn't have to.

As he approached, Sassy danced away.

Rather than chase the horse down, Gavin took a step back. "I would have helped you down…"

Aurelia chuckled. "She's not quite ready for male interaction. She'll need more time for that." She slid out of the saddle and nimbly dropped to the ground.

Gavin led his horse through the trees to a stream and allowed Ranger to drink.

Aurelia brought Sassy to the water as well. "It's beautiful here."

"I've always thought so."

"You've been to other countries…" Aurelia stated. He had to have been if he'd been a Navy SEAL. "How does Montana compare?"

"Of the countries I've seen so far, none are as beautiful as Montana."

Aurelia didn't let his comment bother her. She had to agree that Montana was breathtaking. But there were other beautiful places in the world. Montana wasn't the only one. She bent to scoop water up in her hand. "Have you been to Europe?"

"A couple of times, but we didn't stay long. Usually stopped in Germany on our way to the Middle East."

"Did you have a chance to see much in Germany?"

"Not much outside the airport. We did get to eat in Frankfurt once. I remember the buildings being picturesque. And lots of flowers in window boxes. I wouldn't mind going back and exploring more. I love history, and there's so much of it in Europe."

Some of the tension in her shoulders relaxed. He was game for travel. Some people didn't want to leave home. Ever. "I love to travel." She straightened and glanced around as a breeze ruffled the leaves above, making the stream sparkle with the dappled sunlight. "Each country has its own beauty."

"Have you been many places?" he asked.

She nodded. "A few." Too many to count. She'd gone to many diplomatic events with her parents, traveling to various countries to learn more about them and to educate them on the tiny country of Lastovia. Small countries tended to get lost next to the larger ones with constant news coverage and economic impact.

Gavin tied Ranger to a tree and removed the saddle bag from behind the saddle. "Hungry?"

As she tied Sassy to the tree beside Ranger, Aurelia's stomach rumbled. "Surprisingly, yes." She glanced up at the gap between the trees to the sun shining overhead. "I can't believe it's already close to noon. Time flies when you're out in the sunshine. Are we eating here?"

"No. We have a little more of a hike to do on foot. Are you up for it?"

"I'm ready," she said. She wondered how able he was with a prosthetic leg.

He slung the saddle bag over his shoulder then held out his hand.

Aurelia slid hers inside his and let him lead her on a path that followed the creek upstream. As they climbed over rocks and weaved in between brush, ducking low to avoid tree branches, she could hear the increasing sound of water rushing. But the stream seemed calm, burbling beside them. What could make that much noise?

Her curiosity piqued, Aurelia couldn't wait to round the outcropping of rocks.

And she wasn't disappointed.

She gasped when the source of the rushing noise came into view. Over forty feet high, a narrow waterfall fell in a curtain of shimmering liquid into a wide, blue pool that ultimately fed the stream they'd followed to find the magical place.

The beauty of the water, the trees and the entire setting stole her breath away. "Brilliant," she said in a soft voice.

Gavin chuckled. "I'm glad you like it. This is where we're going to have our picnic."

"I can't imagine another place more perfect." And she couldn't. No wonder he loved Montana so much. With hidden gems like this, who would ever want to leave? Sadness slipped in to her consciousness, stealing some of the joy of the day. "Thank you for bringing me here."

Gavin pulled a blanket out of one side of the saddle bag.

Together, they spread it out on a smooth rock and sat cross-legged in the middle.

Gavin removed the water bottles and the sandwiches. "I hope you like roast beef on wheat."

"I do," she said.

"Mustard or mayo?" he asked.

"Mustard."

"A woman after my own heart," he said and

handed her the sandwich with the mustard. "Do you like spicy foods?"

"I do. Indian curry, sushi with wasabi and Mexican habanero sauces are my favorites."

"We have something in common. I like food that challenges my taste buds. And I'm not afraid to try things that are different."

Aurelia grinned. "That's good. When you travel, you can't always get your tried and true favorites."

"Exactly." He bit into his sandwich and chewed awhile.

Aurelia took a bite of her own and tried to think of how she could bring up the truth about why she wanted to marry—and soon. She turned over different ways to present it, going over and over each scenario in her mind while eating her sandwich. She decided that after they finished lunch would be better than disrupting their meal. So, she ate every bite slowly, knowing she was procrastinating. She didn't want the quiet, intimate moment to end.

After she shoved the last bite into her mouth, she knew it was time to confess. She stared down at her hands, trying to come up with the right words that wouldn't make him so angry he'd call everything off and send her packing.

"You have mustard on your fingers," Gavin said.

She focused, noting the yellow stain on her finger. "Good grief," she said and leaped to her feet.

"Where are you going?"

"To wash the mustard off my hand." She grimaced. "I can imagine it's all over my face as well?"

"I wouldn't say all over," Gavin said.

Sweet truffles. How was she going to have a heart-to-heart conversation with Gavin if she had mustard on her face, detracting from her credibility? She leaped to her feet, her cheeks on fire. "I'll be right back."

"Where are you going?"

"To wash the mustard off my hands, face and anywhere else it might be that I don't know about. Then, we need to talk." She hurried toward the edge of the pool, embarrassed and nervous about the talk they would have once she wasn't covered in mustard.

Gavin chuckled and rose to his feet. "You only have mustard on your finger, that I could see."

"I'm known for being a bit of a mess," she said and squatted down beside the pool, peering at her reflection in the water. If only she had a mirror.

Aurelia rubbed her hands together beneath the surface, scrubbing the mustard from her fingers. Then she reached down to scoop up water in her palms to splash on her face. Her foot slipped in the soft dirt. When she moved to steady herself, she slipped some more. The next thing she knew she was off balance and falling.

Splash!

Aurelia went under. The water was deeper than she'd anticipated. She scrambled to get her feet beneath her. When at last she did, she pushed to stand, her head rising above the surface. She sucked in a deep breath and pushed wet hair out of her face.

Gavin stood on the bank, his brow furrowed. "I was just about to come in after you. Are you all right?"

She nodded, feeling more like an idiot than ever. All over a spot of mustard on her finger. "The only thing hurt is my pride."

"You should have seen your face when you went in." Gavin's chuckle turned to laughter. "Sorry, but your surprised look was priceless." He reached out a hand, his lips still twitching at the corners.

Aurelia took his extended hand. When he started to pull up, she pulled with a hard jerk that sent him flying forward and into the water beside her.

When he came up spluttering, she cocked an eyebrow and smiled. "You should have seen the surprise on your face when you fell in."

He shook his head like a dog, water slinging left and right from his hair. "Oh, no, you didn't."

She tilted her head and smirked. "Oh, yes, I did."

Gavin bent low in the water and wrestled with something. A moment later, he lifted a boot out of the water and turned it upside down to empty it, and then set it on the rock near their picnic blanket.

Aurelia grimaced, hoping she hadn't ruined the leather of his boots.

He worked even harder to get the other boot off his prosthetic foot.

"Don't think we're not going to have that talk you mentioned," Gavin said. "Just give me a minute." He laid the other boot beside the first and reached for the button on his jeans.

Aurelia's eyes widened, and heat coiled low in her belly.

"It's about to get real here," he said. "I have to get my prosthetic off and let it dry."

"Oh, Gavin, I'm sorry. I didn't think about what the water might do to your leg." She swam over to him. "What can I do to help?"

"I need to get out of my jeans in order to remove the leg." He smirked. "And no, this isn't just an excuse to get naked and make love to you." He captured her cheek in his palm and bent to brush a light kiss across her lips. "Although the thought is intriguing."

Feeling like a complete idiot, Aurelia reached for the waistband of his jeans. "I can help," she said and dragged the wet denim over his hips and down his legs. He leaned back and raised his hips, paddling with his arms to keep his head above the water.

As she struggled with the jeans, he fought to stay afloat, all the while laughing.

"I'm so sorry," Aurelia said. "And I don't understand what's so funny." When at last she had his jeans off, she stood in the water and twisted the denim, wringing the water out of them.

"The situation. Here I'm trying to be a gentleman and treat you right…"

"And I'm anything but a lady, dragging you into the water without giving a thought to your leg." She spread the jeans out on the rock and turned back.

He had the prosthetic leg off, holding it out of the water. He hopped to the water's edge and dumped the water out of the socket.

"Is it ruined?" she asked.

"No, but it needs to dry before I can wear it again." He laid it in the sun and stripped what appeared to be a kind of sock off his stump and spread it out in the sun as well. "Thankfully, I had the good sense to wear boxers today. Normally, I go commando." He winked and pulled his T-shirt over his head and flung it onto the rocks. "Now that we're in the water, we might as well enjoy it. Come on. The waterfall is amazing." He pushed backward and did a backstroke away from her.

Aurelia pulled her boots off and laid them on the rocks near his. Because her jeans were weighing her down, she dragged them off, wrung them out and spread them over the rock. Then she pulled her shirt over her head and did the same with it. She wore a bra and panties. And what was a bikini anyway, but a bra and panties? Deliciously unencumbered, she swam after Gavin, loving the coolness of the water on the hot day.

Gavin stopped beside the waterfall and pulled himself from the water to sit on a rock.

Aurelia tread water nearby, appreciating the view. Gavin had a broad chest with a smattering of curly hairs scattered between small dark brown nipples. Powerful arms lifted to the sky, embracing the cool water showering down on him.

Aurelia licked her lips, wanting more than anything to taste those nipples and flick the little nubs with her tongue. Her core tightened. Swimming closer, she pulled herself up onto a rock beside him and lifted her face to the spray. She couldn't remember ever being so free and uninhibited. Had she been back in her country, paparazzi would have found her and snapped pictures of her in her underwear, and then plastered the images all over the news and tabloids.

In Montana, she wasn't Princess Olivia of Lastovia. She was Aurelia, a lonely woman willing to marry a stranger in a mail-order bride deal.

Big hands gripped her shoulder and pulled her close. "Do you know what you're doing to me?" he whispered into her ear.

"Nothing more than you're doing to me. Turnabout is fair play," she said, blinking up at him in the water's spray.

He cupped her chin and bent to kiss her, the taste of the cool, clean water on his mouth and tongue as he slid between her teeth in a tender, but sensuous caress.

Aurelia threaded her hands together behind his neck and pressed her breasts against his chest. She couldn't get close enough, and their perch was somewhat precarious.

Gavin slipped slightly, broke away from the kiss and muttered a curse. He slipped into the water, captured her hand and swam toward the shallower end of the pool. Once he had his foot on the ground and she could stand as well with her head well above the surface, he resumed the kiss. His hand traveled down to the small of her back, sliding beneath the waistband of her panties to cup her ass.

Aurelia moaned into his mouth. With one foot on the bottom of the pool, she helped him maintain balance while she raised her other leg. She wrapped it around his waist, rubbing her center across his hip. She wanted more. Much more than a kiss. Sliding her hand into the waistband of his boxers, she cupped his bottom and squeezed, digging her nails into his skin, pressing him closer.

His erection nudged her belly, proof he was as aroused as she.

What was stopping her? They were alone, up in the mountains of Montana. Who would know or care besides them? And if they were going to marry, didn't they owe it to themselves to know whether they were sexually compatible?

Beyond giving a damn, Aurelia reached behind her back and unclipped her bra. The lacy fabric floated up to the surface.

Gavin slipped the straps from her arms and slung the garment across the rocks to where their other clothes lay drying in the sun.

Aurelia pushed his shorts down over his hips and lower. Taking a breath, she lowered her head beneath the water and skimmed her hand along his muscular thigh, dragging the last piece of his clothing down to his ankle. Holding onto her shoulders for balance, he kicked it free.

She grabbed them and slung them to join her bra on the rocks. Then in a lightning move, she stripped out of her panties and stood before him naked, wet and burning with desire.

Gavin leaned one hand against the rocky outcropping. With the other, he cupped her ass and brought her legs up around his waist. Then he leaned her back against the ledge. "I wasn't supposed to get this far today. I was supposed to take my time, show you respect, be gentle and considerate." He kissed the side of her neck below her earlobe, and then dragged his lips across her chin. "I'm failing miserably at this dating thing. We're supposed to get to know each other before we take it all the way."

Aurelia captured his face between her hands, her channel poised above his hardened cock. "Says who?" And she kissed his cheek, the tip of his nose, and then his lips as she lowered herself over him, taking his length inside her.

"I don't remember now," he said. "I barely remember my name when you do that."

"Gavin," she whispered.

"Aurelia," he responded and thrust upward, pushing deeper until he filled her completely, stretching her channel with his deliciously thick shaft. "We were supposed to talk," he said into her mouth.

"We will...after." She rose up and lowered again. This was where she'd wanted to be. "Forget everything but us. Here. Now."

"Forgotten," he said and moaned. Gavin gripped her hips and thrust into her, again and again, closing his eyes, his face tense, his body stiffening with every movement.

Aurelia's insides, tightened around him, pulling him deeper, urging him to give his all. Tingling sensations started at her core and rocketed outward, spreading to the very tips of her fingers and toes. She clung to him, riding the force of her climax.

Gavin thrust once more and held her close, buried deep inside, as his cock throbbed and jerked. Then he pulled free, his breath catching, his heart pounding against her fingertips. "Damn!" he said.

Laughter bubbled up her throat and escaped. "Not exactly the reaction I would have expected after that."

He rested his forehead against hers, his breathing coming in rapid gulps. "I forgot. How stupid of me."

"Forgot what?" she asked.

He lifted his head and stared into her eyes. "Protection."

She froze, her heart sliding to a screeching halt. "Damn."

"I pulled out before I came," he said. "At least, I think I did soon enough." He shoved a hand through his wet hair, standing it on end. "Hell, I blew it. I was supposed to wait. I didn't even bring anything. This wasn't supposed to happen."

"Do you regret it?" Aurelia smoothed a hand along his temple and brushed her lips across his. "I don't."

"We haven't even talked or gotten to know each other."

She smiled. "We got to know something about each other."

Gavin drew in a deep breath. "And it was amazing."

"Yes, it was," she said. "But you're right. We still need to talk. I need to tell you about me, and what you're getting into if you decide to marry me."

"I think I know all I need to know, after that. We're most definitely sexually compatible."

She nodded and dropped her legs to the bottom of the pool. "We are. But there's more to me than just a woman to make love to."

"I know that you're an amazing horsewoman. And you're patient with difficult animals and men." He smoothed his hand along her shoulder and down to her hand, lifting it up to his lips. "What more do I need to know?"

She opened her palm and pressed it against the side of his face. Then she drew a deep breath. "I haven't given you the full disclosure. I'm not who you think I am."

CHAPTER 12

"Full disclosure?" Gavin's brow dipped and a lead weight settled in the pit of his belly. "What could be so bad that I wouldn't want to be with you? The mail-order bride site vets their applicants. You didn't show up in their criminal screening. You haven't committed a felony, have you?"

She smiled and shook her head. "No. I'm not a criminal."

"They also screen to make sure applicants aren't married and cheating. You're not married already, are you?"

She shook her head. "I've never married. When I have been engaged, my prospective grooms have died tragically."

His frown deepened. "Grooms? You've been engaged more than once?"

She nodded. "Twice."

His eyebrows twisted. "Did you kill your fiancés?" he asked, but he couldn't imagine Aurelia having that wicked a bone in her body.

"No," she said. "Someone else killed them."

"Why?" he asked.

"Because someone doesn't want me to marry."

"I repeat...why?" He stood in front of her, treading water, wanting answers.

Her gaze fell away. "We should get dressed, and then I'll answer all your questions."

"Damn right, you will." He started for the shallower water near the bank when a shot rang out.

"What the hell?" Gavin ducked automatically, grabbed Aurelia's arm and pulled her low in the water, ducking behind the rocky outcropping they'd just made love against. He pushed her behind him, keeping her hidden in the shadows cast by the stone ledge.

More bullets flew past them. One hit the rocks above him, ricocheting into the water near to where they stood. He wanted to fly out of the water and go after whoever was shooting at them, but he couldn't. Not without his leg. He couldn't put it on without getting out of the water and leaving Aurelia alone, and whenever Gavin leaned out, away from the rocky outcropping, more shots were fired, getting closer and closer. He stopped leaning out. If someone wanted to push the envelope, they'd have to come to him. He didn't have his leg, and he couldn't go chasing anyone on a leg and a stump.

"How?" Aurelia crossed her arms over her breasts and sank low in the water. "How did they find me?"

"What do you mean, *how did they find you?*'

"I was trying to tell you. Anyone I promised to marry has ended up dead."

"Why would someone not want you to marry?" A bullet clinked off the rocks above Gavin. He ducked instinctively. "This is insane. We have to get out of here." He reached his arm over the top of the rock, feeling for his prosthesis.

Several more gunshots echoed off the hills, seeming to be closer.

Gavin couldn't wait for the gunman to get right up on them. He could think of only one other place they could hide. "How long can your hold your breath under water?"

Aurelia shook her head. "I don't know. A minute, maybe two? Why?"

"We have to make a break for it. If we stay here, that gunman might come over and finish the job. We're unarmed, defenseless. Our only option is to hide."

"Where?" She trembled, gooseflesh rising on her naked skin.

Gavin nodded toward the waterfall. "Behind the curtain of the falls, there's a shallow cave. If we could swim underwater all the way to the falls, we can hide back there until the gunman leaves."

Aurelia stared across the open expanse of water, chewing her lip.

More gunfire made her jump.

"Okay. Let's do it."

Gavin reached again for his prosthesis, found it and his stump sock and pulled them over the ledge. A bullet just barely missed his hand. He shoved the items into a crack in the rocks. When the shooter was gone, he'd have to return for his leg. There was a good chance they'd have to walk back to the ranch.

Once he had the leg and sock secured, he glanced at Aurelia, naked and shivering. "Are you ready?"

She nodded, her teeth chattering. "I'm r-ready."

"Stay as close to the bottom as you can and don't release any air. Bubbles will give us away." Gavin glanced at the sun, now angling across the trees, casting shadows over the pool. "Follow me." He sank low in the water, drew in a deep breath and went under at the same time as Aurelia. Together, they pushed off the rocks to get a good start through the open water. Then they were swimming as fast as they could go, staying as close to the bottom as they could. With every stroke, their bodies tried to rise to the surface.

As they neared the falls, Gavin took the lead, guiding Aurelia through the maze of boulders littering the base of the falls.

Finally, Gavin burst through the bubbling rush of water tumbling into the pool from the falls above. He rose to the surface, just enough to be sure he couldn't be seen through the veil of water. Then he snagged Aurelia's arm and dragged her up beside him.

She surfaced, gasping for air. For a full minute, she dragged in deep, lungs full of air. When she could finally breathe normally, she stared at the sheet of water. "Are you sure he can't see us?" she asked.

"If we can't see out, he can't see in. And we have the added bonus of being in the shadows of the cave."

Aurelia wrapped her arms around herself. "How long do you think he'll be out there?"

"I don't know. We might have to stay hidden until dark."

A violent shiver wracked her body.

"We need to get you out of the water and dried off." Gavin grabbed onto a tree root and pulled himself out of the water onto the bank leading up into the shallow cave. He reached out and pulled Aurelia up beside him. "Can you get yourself up into the dry part of the cave?"

She nodded and started to rise. As she straightened—naked beautiful and chilled—she took his arm, looped it over her shoulder and helped him to his feet. Not a word was spoken between them as they worked their way up the slope.

Once they reached dry dirt, Gavin eased himself

to the ground and held out his hand. "This isn't exactly how I pictured our day ending," he muttered.

She let him draw her down to sit beside him. He pulled her into his arms and held her close. "The only way to get warm when you're naked is to share body heat with someone else. I promise, my plan today wasn't to get you naked." He held her close and prayed his body's natural reaction to hers would remain at bay until they had a chance to make love again in a bed, not a pool or on the dirt. He wanted to show her how beautiful it could be to make love like normal people.

Hell, there was nothing normal about what had happened this day.

"Talk to me, Aurelia," Gavin said. "Tell me what's going on."

She stiffened in his arms. "Please, don't hate me."

His hold tightened along with the knot in his gut. "I won't hate you."

"You will be angry." Aurelia sighed. "And I won't blame you. I should have been completely upfront with you from the beginning."

"I'm not a very patient man," he said, his voice more abrupt than he intended.

"Okay. Here goes." She took a deep breath. "I'm not just Aurelia George. I'm Olivia Aurelia St. George." She gave a mirthless laugh. "Princess of Lastovia." She laughed again, the sound ending on a sob. "As I'm sitting here in the dirt, naked and exposed, it seems impossible, but there you have it. I'm a princess, the last in the direct line for the throne of Lastovia, a very small country in Europe. You probably hadn't heard of it before the news report last night."

Gavin closed his eyes and shook his head. "You're the missing princess." His arm tightened around her. "So far, I'm not mad. Shocked. But not mad."

"I hadn't gotten to that part yet," she whispered.

"Go on." His arm loosened around her.

"My parents and my older brother died in a car crash two years ago. My brother was supposed to be the next in line for the throne. Not me. I was never intended to be the queen."

"Until both your parents and your brother died in the crash. I'm sorry for your loss. That had to be hard." He pulled her close and stroked a hand down her back.

She nodded. "It was horrible. We were close. I have no one else that close."

"No cousins, aunts, uncles?"

"Some second and third cousins, twice removed. But no other family I'm really close to. But I'm not asking for pity."

"So, now you're in line for the throne?" he said softly, encouraging her to continue.

She nodded. "But, as with many monarchies with parliaments in place to make and carry out laws, they have rules for the ruling class. For me to take the crown, I must marry and bear a child before my thirtieth birthday." When she stopped talking, the sound of the water falling seemed to be amplified to a roar.

That anger she'd spoken of started low in Gavin's gut and radiated outward like a slow burn. "Let me get this straight. You said you were engaged twice before."

She nodded. "Yes."

"And both men died."

"One died in a crash, much like my parents. The other was knocked out into the street and run over by a bus."

"Did you love either one of them?" Gavin asked.

Aurelia's back straightened. "It is not always necessary to love in order to fulfill one's obligation."

Gavin's jaw clenched. "I'll take that as a no."

"No," she said. "But I did not wish ill on either one of them. They were good men."

"And now you're in another country, willing to marry a stranger to fulfill your obligation," he said, keeping his voice even.

She stiffened. "I had to leave Lastovia and hide away long enough to marry."

"And have a child?"

She nodded. "As I stated in my response to your ad, my biological clock is ticking, and it is. Along with my government's deadline. I must marry and produce an heir before I turn thirty in ten months or the throne goes to my cousin Rupert."

"And that's a bad thing?"

"You would only have to meet Rupert to know how bad it would be. He doesn't care about our people, only about himself. He would not represent our country well with the world. The man is so greedy, he would bankrupt our country within a year of becoming king. I can't let that happen to my people."

"So, you chose me to be your chump husband, a man desperate enough to resort to a mail-order bride." He snorted. "I should have known a beautiful woman like you would have an ulterior motive for resorting to becoming a mail-order bride."

She nodded. "You met all the criteria. You needed a bride, you lived in a faraway place. I could hide in Montana until we were married and well on our way to having our first child." Her voice faded off. "And you had a very handsome face with eyes that…well… spoke to me."

"I met your criteria. I was a desperate man, willing to go to a website to get a wife," Gavin clarified. Once again, the sound of the waterfall seemed to roar in Gavin's ears.

"I'm sorry. I should have told you the whole truth from the beginning." Aurelia touched his arm with her cold fingers. "But if I had, would you have given me a chance? Would you have wanted to get to know me better?"

"You didn't give me the benefit of a doubt," he

said. His chest felt so tight, he could barely breathe. "All this time, you just wanted any man who could give you a child."

"At first, that was true. But then I met you." She leaned into him. "Sounds trite, but I thought I might have it all. Save my birth right, have the children I want and a man I had come to care for." She laughed again, the sound ending on a sob. "I guess it was too much to ask for. I'm sorry I used you. You deserve better."

Gavin didn't respond. The anger was still there, but with her naked body pressed against his, he couldn't think straight enough. He needed a chance to get away from her, to clear his mind and figure out what he wanted and how Aurelia fit into it.

Then a thought occurred to him. "Where does Collin fit into this picture. He didn't just show up to take the ranch hand position, did he?"

She shook her head. "He's my bodyguard."

"Why didn't you just marry him?"

"I couldn't. I know him too well. He's not in love with me, nor am I in love with him."

"It was easier to choose someone you didn't know?" Gavin laughed. "Princess, you have a crazy way of thinking."

"I know. This whole situation wasn't supposed to happen. I was supposed to be footloose, traveling the world doing philanthropy work for my people, building good will around the world, spreading the word that our country exists." Tears slipped down her cheeks, and she brushed them away. "I don't mind giving up my dream of traveling. I'd give it up in a heartbeat to have my family back."

His heart wrenched at the sadness in her voice. But he wasn't ready to forgive her, yet. He didn't like that she'd planned to use him. "What about our child? Were you just going to take him away to your country? Would I have had no say in the matter?"

"I'd hoped by the time we got to know and trust each other that we could come to an agreement. Our child wouldn't have to be raised in Lastovia. *She* could live her life in Montana."

"But one day, *he'd* rule your country? Wouldn't *his* people want to know *him*? Wouldn't it be right for *him* to know them?"

Her lips twitched as she nodded. "Whether the baby is a he or a she, yes. Again. I hadn't even gotten that far. I was working toward my birthday." Aurelia sighed. "What does it matter, now? Rupert will take the throne. Perhaps I'm wrong, and he'll be a good king. I can only hope."

Though he was mad at the entire situation, Gavin held onto Aurelia, keeping her as warm as he could while they waited out the gunman. She dozed off a couple of times, jerking away when her dreams turned to nightmares. He liked holding her in his arms, but he wasn't sure he could buy into her plight or the fact she'd withheld vital information. He needed time to process.

Darkness settled in the mountains earlier than on the plains. Soon, the little sunlight that had warmed the area around the pool had disappeared.

Gavin gently shook Aurelia awake. "I'm going to check and see if the gunman is gone."

Her pulse leaped and she held onto his arm. "I'm going with you."

"It would be safer for you, if you stayed here," he said.

"The same goes for you," she shot back. "It's because of me that anyone is shooting at you." She pushed to her feet and looped his arm over her shoulder. Naked and cold, she refused to remain behind while this man who'd protected her put his life on the line again. "Come on, big guy. Let's go for a swim."

She helped him down to the water.

With the warmth of the sun gone, the water was cool and stole Aurelia's breath away. But she didn't hesitate as she slipped in up to her neck. With darkness shrouding the pool, they didn't have to swim underwater. Instead, they emerged from the waterfall and breaststroked slowly across the pool to the rocky ledge where they'd left their clothing to dry.

"I'm going to crawl out onto the shore and look

around. Please, stay here," Gavin whispered. "I'm a trained warrior. You aren't. I'd rather go it alone rather than lose focus worrying about you."

Aurelia didn't like the idea of him going out there on his own, but he made a good point. With her going along with him, she'd make him vulnerable. "Okay, I'll give you one minute then I'm coming out."

"Two."

She hesitated. "Two."

"When I signal, hand me my leg, will ya?"

"I will," she responded.

Gavin pulled himself up onto the shore and low-crawled across the ground to crouch in the shadow of a bush. He waited there quietly listening for any sounds of movement, the clink of metal or the whisper of voices.

After a full minute, he heard nothing but the sound of frogs and crickets singing in the night, undisturbed by the intrusion of humans.

Before the second minute was up, Gavin scooted himself over to the edge of the rock ledge and leaned over. "Leg."

His prosthetic swung over the edge nearly clipping him in the side of his head.

"Is it clear?" she whispered.

"So far as I can tell."

He slipped the sleeve over his stump and pulled on the prosthetic.

By the time he had his leg on, Aurelia had climbed

out of the water and stood dripping beside him. "Where are our clothes?"

"I don't know." Gavin pushed to his feet and adjusted his leg in the device. Then he looked around. Their clothes weren't where they'd left them. He expanded his search until he determined they weren't going to find them, their boots, blanket or saddle bag.

In the chill night air, it wouldn't be long before hypothermia set in.

"What do you want to bet the horses are gone as well," Aurelia said, her arms crossed over her breasts, her teeth chattering.

"I'm not taking that bet, because I think you're right."

"Well, we can't stand around waiting for our limousine to arrive." Aurelia held out her hand for Gavin. "I hope you can find your way back to the ranch house in the dark."

"I'm not sure it's a good idea to try to walk all the way back barefooted." He squeezed her hand in his. "This is bear country. And they tend to be nocturnal."

Aurelia moved closer to Gavin. "What do we do? Should we climb up a tree and wait for someone to come looking for us?"

"Climbing a tree won't help. Black bears are great climbers."

"Way to burst my city-girl bubble." Aurelia looked around in the limited light from the emerging stars.

"What do you propose?" She'd never imagined she'd be stranded in the wilderness, naked as the day she was born.

"We can start down the mountain, but we might have to hole up for the night along the way. Your feet probably aren't tough enough to go far without shoes."

Already the stones and rocks were digging into the soft soles of her feet. "I can make it," she said, refusing to hold them back from reaching civilization. "Can you walk on your prosthesis without a boot?"

"It's not recommended, but I can."

"Any advice on avoiding bears?" she asked, her voice accompanied by the chatter of her teeth.

"Don't wrestle one? If you see a baby bear, get the hell away from it. Where there's a baby, there's a protective mama close by."

"Anything else I should be afraid of? Because as beautiful as this state is, I'm not appreciating some of its drawbacks right now."

"Watch out for rattlesnakes."

Aurelia shook violently between the chill and the thought of snakes. She didn't think she could stop her body from trembling. Still, they couldn't just sit and freeze. Moving was their only option. "Let's go. Damn the bears and snakes. I want a bath, clothing and a stiff drink when we get to the house."

Keeping her goals in mind, Aurelia, stripped of

her clothing, her horse and her pride, walked down the mountain trail silently cursing the sharp-edged stones she stepped on and gripping Gavin's hand to keep from falling over the side of a cliff.

They had traveled what felt like a dozen miles, but in actuality was probably only a half a mile when the sounds of engines echoing off the sides of the mountains made them duck into the bushes alongside the trail.

Minutes later, three four-wheelers roared up the trail toward them, headlights blazing the path ahead.

"Stay down," Gavin said.

The ATVs moved slowly up the narrow trail. When one came close enough, Gavin said, "That's Percy." He leaped to his feet and waved.

Aurelia remained hunkered low in the bush, thrilled that they'd been found, but not willing to jump up like Gavin and expose herself to the riders.

Percy pulled to a stop and got off the vehicle. "Blackstock, what the hell happened? Shit, man, where are your clothes?"

Collin leaped off the second vehicle and ran to where Gavin stood. "Where's the prin—Aurelia?" he demanded.

"The princess is right behind me," he said, his tone dry. "But we were caught unawares by a gunman. Give me your jacket." He held out his hand.

Collin tried to look past Gavin. "Aurelia? Are you okay?"

"I'm fine, but cold. Do as Gavin asked and give him your jacket."

Collin stripped out of his jacket and handed it over.

Gavin turned and handed it to Aurelia.

She pulled it on, zipped the front and finally stood, the jacket covering everything from her neck to her knees. "Thank you."

While Aurelia was dressing, Percy stripped his shirt off and handed it to Gavin, who slipped it over his shoulders and buttoned the front. It didn't cover much, but it covered enough to get him back to the ranch.

Lori pulled up on the ATV behind Collin. "Thank God, we found you two. When the horses returned without their riders, we were worried. I told them we'd find you up near the waterfall. Here, you two can have my ride. I'll double up with Percy."

"Ride with me," Collin said. "Let Percy lead the way. You and I can bring up the rear."

Lori's eyes narrowed. "Only if I get to drive. The trails are tricky."

"Deal. You drive." He pulled a handgun from his shoulder holster. "I'll cover the princess—Aurelia."

Lori frowned. "What's all this about a princess?"

"I'll fill you in when we get back to the house," Gavin said.

Glad she would be riding back with Gavin, Aurelia slipped on behind the man and wrapped her arms tightly around his waist. Soon, they were easing down the mountain path at a pace that would make a tortoise seem fast. But it was fine with Aurelia, as long as they arrived in one piece and she didn't have to step on one more rock to get there.

Cold and beyond exhausted, she couldn't even worry about what would happen tomorrow. Her focus was on not falling off the back of the ATV and surviving long enough to reach the house and a hot bath. She'd worry about where her life would go next when she wasn't afraid she might not live through the night between gunmen, snakes, bears and killer cliffs.

CHAPTER 13

"WANNA FILL me in on what the hell happened last night?" Percy asked the next morning at the kitchen table.

"I told you last night, a gunman fired on us while we were swimming up by the waterfall."

"Yeah, tell us all about it. Like why you ended up wearing Percy's shirt back." Franklin grinned.

"And nothing else," Vasquez added.

"Talk about getting caught with your pants down," Young piped in.

Gavin slammed his fist on the table. "Shut the fuck up. It's none of your goddamn business what we were or weren't wearing. The point is, someone was trying to make Swiss cheese out of us."

Lori tapped her fingernail against the tabletop. "Where's the princess now."

"Princess?" Vasquez's brow puckered.

"Aurelia," Lori said. "She's a real-life, honest-to-God princess."

"Princess of what?" Young asked.

"A tiny European country called Lastovia," Lori said. "I had to look it up on a map. It's like Monaco. So small you have to enlarge the map to see it. It's even smaller than Idaho."

"What the hell's she doing in Montana?" Vasquez asked.

"Husband hunting," Lori said. "And I'm sorry I got you into this, Gavin."

Gavin shoved a hand through his hair. "It's not your fault. I'm the idiot that let it happen."

Percy shook his head. "I feel like I need subtext for this conversation. Please, give the old man all the words."

Lori rolled her eyes. "I set Gavin up on a mail-order bride site. He got the princess."

"Wow! Talk about hitting the jackpot." Franklin gave Vasquez a high five. "Where do we sign up for our own princesses?"

"You don't." Lori pointed a finger at the two young men. "You see where it got Gavin."

"Naked in the waterfall pool, from where I see it," Young said, his grin splitting his face.

"And being shot at," Lori reminded him. "She came to Montana to marry Gavin so she can have his baby and go back to her country to assume the throne."

Franklin stared at Gavin, one eyebrow cocked. "And you're not happy because...?"

"Because she used me," Gavin admitted. "She didn't come here because she cared. She came because I was a man. She needed a man to marry and give her a baby."

"But you signed up for a mail-order bride," Percy pointed out. "You needed a woman. You didn't know her or care about her before you met. You wanted a bride and children. How's that not using her?"

"It's different," Gavin insisted. But when Percy put it that way, it made him just as guilty. But he wouldn't have taken the child away to a foreign country and left his wife alone. Wasn't that what Aurelia had planned? Have a kid and then leave Gavin, taking the kid to her country to raise?

"So, Blackstock..." Percy crossed his arms over his chest. "What are you going to do?"

"I've been thinking..."

Franklin's brow dipped. "That's a dangerous thing."

"What did you come up with? Are you going to send the princess packing?"

"No," Gavin said.

"What are you going to do with her?" Vasquez asked.

"I'd like to know that as well," a female voice said from the door leading into the living room. "What are you going to do with me?" Aurelia entered the room, dark circles beneath her eyes. "I'm packed and ready to go, if you want to take me into Bozeman to catch the first plane back to Lastovia."

"No," Gavin said. He didn't want her to go. Not yet. He hadn't completely sorted through his feelings for the woman. But he'd made up his mind about one thing. "You're staying. And we're getting married."

A collective gasp sounded from everyone in the room but Gavin.

"Tomorrow," he added.

"You can't get married that quickly in Montana," Hannah walked into the room at that moment. "Women under 50 have to have proof of a rubella blood test."

"Then Aurelia gets one this morning. We get the marriage license this afternoon, and we're getting married tomorrow." Gavin pushed to his feet and faced Aurelia. "That's what you wanted, wasn't it? Get married and have a baby before you turn thirty?"

Aurelia stared at him, the circles beneath her eyes seeming to darken as he watched. She gave a brief nod but didn't voice an answer.

"Then what are we waiting for? We have to plan a wedding." He clapped his hands together. "Let's get going."

Aurelia shook her head. "Why?"

"Why what?" He stopped in front of her. "You wanted to get married. I'm offering to do the job. What more do you want?"

"You could have proposed," Hannah said, softly. "Like a decent man would do."

"She doesn't need a proposal or a decent man. She just needs a man who can give her children." He captured Aurelia's gaze with a hard one of his own. "Am I right?"

Her back straightened, and she lifted her chin. "Yes."

"Then let's get to town for a blood test and a marriage license. I'm betting the gunman from yesterday will still be around. We can kill two birds with one stone by getting married tomorrow. We meet your deadline, and we catch the bastard who tried to kill us. For that, I'll need a little help from all of you, and we can stack our guest list with anyone Hank Patterson can spare from the Brotherhood Protectors."

Percy grinned. "Now, you're talking. We have to catch the bastard who tried to kill you two."

"We want him alive, if possible." Gavin's eyes narrowed to slits. "If he's not the one behind the deaths of Aurelia's former fiancés and her parents, he might give us the name of the guy who hired him to do the job here."

Hannah squared her shoulders. "Looks like we'll have a wedding here at Brighter Days. If we're going to make it happen, we'd better get moving. I won't let our princess have anything less than a wedding fit for a queen." She turned to Lori. "Get Sadie McClain on the phone. If she's not on a movie set, she'll be a huge asset getting this show on the road. While you're at it, have Hank dedicate some of his Brotherhood Protectors to the ranch for the duration. I'll get a hold of the sheriff and inform him of the shooting."

"Phone Hank and Sadie. Got it. And I'll call Allie, Hank's sister," Lori said. "She's gone through wedding planning as well. We'll get this party rolling."

Hannah nodded. "Be ready to make a run to Bozeman with Gavin and Aurelia. We'll need to do some emergency dress shopping and rent a tux for the groom."

Gavin stared at Hannah and Lori, appalled at what they were planning. "What's wrong with a simple wedding wearing jeans and a T-shirt?"

Hannah planted a fist on her hip. "You want this to look like a real wedding, or not?"

"And as far as that goes, we should put the word out." Lori's eyes brightened. "Sadie might know someone in the media who can get a reporter here to cover the princess bride's marriage."

"What about your family?" Hannah asked Aurelia. "Can they get here by tomorrow afternoon?"

Aurelia shook her head, her eyes glazing.

"She doesn't have any family," Gavin answered for her, seeing the flash of pain in Aurelia's blue eyes.

"What about close friends?"

"Lilianna," she said. "She's my closest friend."

Hannah handed her a telephone. "Call her. See if she can be on the next flight out of…where was it?"

"Lastovia," everyone else answered as one.

Hannah laughed. "Well, we have less than a day to get this wedding together. I'll call everyone I can think of to get the catering, music, tent, flowers and lighting. Oh, and we'll need a preacher." She scanned the room. "Why are you still standing there? Let's do it."

Aurelia stepped out of the room to place her call.

Gavin hadn't thought past saying there would be a wedding tomorrow. The logistics sounded like a nightmare.

Hannah smiled and patted his cheek. "Don't look so shell-shocked. We've got your back. Get to Bozeman and get that blood test and marriage license. Lori, Sadie and I will take Aurelia from there and get what she needs for a wedding. You and your groomsmen will need to get suited up, so don't forget to stop by the tuxedo rental shop. And take your guys with you as bodyguards. Don't come back without your tuxes."

"Yes, ma'am," Gavin said. "I swear my DI in BUD/S training didn't crack the whip as hard as you."

Hannah lifted her chin. "You know I love you, Gavin. Now, move!"

Gavin found himself and Aurelia hustled out of the house and into his truck.

The rest of the men piled into an SUV and followed him out of the yard, promising to have his back in case the gunman tried to take another shot at Gavin and Aurelia.

Hannah wasn't far behind.

As they pulled away, Gavin shot a glance toward Aurelia. "Hannah can be a real ball-buster when she gets on a roll."

Aurelia nodded, her face pale, those eyes seeming to be sunk back in her face.

"Were you able to contact your friend Lilianna?" Gavin asked.

"Yes."

"Is she coming?"

"Yes."

"I also called the Lastovia Prime Minister to let him know what's going on, and that I was okay."

Gavin shot another glance at Aurelia, concerned that she was too quiet and pale. "What's wrong?" he asked, his voice a little harsher than he intended. He blamed it on tension and nerves. Hannah's high-handed takeover of his wedding planning had left his head spinning, making him wonder what the hell he'd just started.

"Who said anything was wrong?" she said, her voice barely above a whisper. She didn't look at him. Instead, she stared straight ahead.

"This is what you wanted. We're getting married. We'll work on getting you pregnant, but I'm telling you now...I will not be cut out of our child's life. Where he goes, I go."

She nodded. "Are you sure this is what you want to do?" This time she faced him, her brow furrowed.

"We're doing it, aren't we?" He took his gaze off the road briefly and studied her face. "Don't tell me you're having second thoughts."

"I've put you in danger," she said, her tone flat, her brow dipping. "I shouldn't have come to Montana."

"But you did. And we're going to flush out your assassin."

"What if the gunman fires into the wedding guests?" She twisted her hands together. "I never wanted anyone to get hurt."

"We'll let everyone know the dangers. They don't have to come."

"I told Lilianna she should stay home." Aurelia snorted softly. "She refused. Said she'd be on the next flight out. She should be here some time tomorrow around noon."

"I'll have Percy pick her up from the airport."

"What else can I say, but thank you," she said weakly. "But I think you're making a big mistake. I'm jinxed. I'm poison to my suitors."

"Whoever killed your previous fiancés hasn't gone up against a Navy SEAL, or any of the Special Forces. Hank Patterson only hires the best of the best for his Brotherhood Protectors. His team will be at the ranch tomorrow. They'll make sure we catch our shooter."

"You're a Navy SEAL. Why didn't you go to work for Hank?"

"I felt like I was needed at Brighter Days. We've had our own challenges. Take you, for instance." He gave her a twisted grimace.

"I should leave before it gets any worse." She touched his arm. "You can take me straight to the airport. Once I leave and the wedding is off, whoever the shooter is will leave you alone."

Gavin shook his head. "But he might go after you."

"I'll take my chances. Collin is my bodyguard. He'll come with me."

His fists clenching around the steering wheel, Gavin fought to keep from driving off the side of the road and pulling Aurelia into his arms and shaking her hard. He didn't want Collin protecting Aurelia. He wanted to be there to make certain no one hurt her. As mad as he was that she hadn't leveled with him, he still couldn't deny the connection building between them. If he wasn't already in love with his princess, he was well on his way to getting there. So, she was a princess. Everyone couldn't be perfect.

AURELIA SAT BESIDE GAVIN, reliving the horror of being shot at the night before, and the terror of something happening equally as despicable as what had happened to her other fiancés. Gavin deserved better. He'd lost a leg fighting for his country. He didn't deserve to lose his life because someone didn't want the princess to marry. It just wasn't right.

When they reached Bozeman, Aurelia walked in a daze from the truck to a lab where they drew her blood and gave her a form stating she'd had her rubella test. With that document in hand along with her real passport, they drove to the county clerk's office and applied for a marriage license. Within minutes, they had that document as well.

Gavin drove her to a bridal shop where Hannah, Lori and two other women were waiting with the owner of the shop, having already pulled several dresses off the rack.

Gavin and the guys would be in the shop next door, trying on tuxedoes. Knowing Gavin wasn't far away made Aurelia a little more comfortable as the ladies ganged up on her and helped her in and out of wedding gowns, until they found the one that suited her the best. Even Aurelia was thrilled with the choice. She would have been happier if she were marrying Gavin because he loved her and she loved him. At least half of that equation was true.

She loved Gavin. For the few short days she'd known him, she'd discovered a man who was true to his word, and honest, courageous and protective of the people he cared about. Any woman would be lucky to have his heart. Aurelia wished it was her.

With a dress chosen and alterations in the works, all they needed now were the shoes, veil and suitable undergarments. The owner of the bridal shop set her up with all of those things.

Hannah, Sadie, Allie and Lori all took turns calling different vendors, arranging for chairs, a tent, catering for the reception, a DJ for the wedding music and reception. Hannah secured a justice of the peace to perform the ceremony. Sadie called a florist who would make an emergency call to all the florists in a 100-mile radius to come up with enough flowers to make the bouquet and decorate the altar. The florist promised to work well into the night to have the arrangements ready by the afternoon wedding.

Aurelia insisted on having the ladies fitted for bridesmaids' dresses. "You all have stepped in to make this a real event. I can't thank you enough." Once they were fitted with dresses of their choice in dusty rose, pastel pink, faded lilac and soft gray, Aurelia selected a pretty dress in petal pink in Lilian-na's size.

By the time they were done, it was late afternoon. The men met them outside the two shops, and they split up into the different vehicles to head back to the ranch.

Dinner was a lively affair with everyone talking about fittings for the tuxedos and dresses, all laughing and joking between each other.

Everything that had happened that day seemed so

surreal, as if it had happened to someone else, not Aurelia. She was getting married the next day, to a man she really loved. And he didn't return the sentiment.

Aurelia went to bed but lay for a long time, wishing she could go to Gavin and have him reassure her that she was doing the right thing for the right reasons. Because as she lay in her bed, she couldn't help but think this was all wrong. She shouldn't marry Gavin just to secure her throne. Gavin deserved to find someone he loved, who would love him in return.

If only he would let that be her.

CHAPTER 14

GAVIN THOUGHT he would lay awake all night thinking about the decision he'd made, worrying if he'd made the right one. But he'd fallen asleep within minutes of laying his head on the pillow. He woke feeling better than he had in years. More optimistic and hopeful for the future. Which was completely strange, considering all he'd learned about Aurelia, or rather, Princess Olivia. As he thought about her, he believed Olivia suited her. She carried herself like a princess, all straight lines and confidence. What was a princess doing with a cowboy like him? Whatever the reason was, he had thrown his hat in the ring. He was going through with the plan.

The sun shone through the window, making him smile. If he was getting married that day, he'd better get up and get the chores done early. He'd need a shower afterward to keep from smelling like one of the barn animals.

Pulling on his leg, jeans, shirt and boots, he was downstairs and out in the barn before anyone else. He checked on Ranger and Sassy. Today, Sassy only tossed her head in his direction when he approached her. She didn't paw a the ground or rear and kick the stall walls.

He was glad to see the mare finally calming down. Aurelia had truly worked her magic on the animal.

Once he had the horses fed, he strode out of the barn, heading for the kitchen.

"You're out awfully early." Percy met him in the yard. "Should you be out in the open today?"

"I took care of the horses. I don't expect anyone to pick up my slack."

"We don't expect you to muck around with animals today. I'll take care of the chickens and pigs. You go inside and see if Cookie needs any help. *And stay inside.* Can't have the groom injured or killed on his wedding day."

A smile tugged at the corners of Gavin's mouth as he entered the house through the kitchen door.

Cookie, skillet in hand, flipped eggs and set them back on the burner.

Gavin glanced around.

"If you're looking for Aurelia, Hannah took her breakfast to her," Cookie said. "You're not supposed to see the bride on your wedding day until the ceremony."

"Who made that dumb rule?" Gavin asked, disappointed he wouldn't see Aurelia all day. He'd gotten used to having her around in the short time she'd been at Brighter Days.

"Not a rule...tradition," Cookie informed him.

"Still, it's dumb." And frustrating. Gavin really wanted to see her, to reassure himself that she was indeed going to go through with the wedding.

"Make yourself useful and man the toaster, Blackstock," Cookie commanded. "Let's get the crew fed so we can clean up the kitchen and get it ready for the afternoon's festivities."

Gavin buttered toast and carried a stack to the table. He helped Cookie get all the usual fixings to the table and set the flatware and plates out for everyone.

Within seconds of the platters being set out, the seats filled, and everyone was reaching for the food.

Gavin caught himself looking for Aurelia several times, wishing she was with him.

Before he knew it, the eggs had been consumed, along with three pounds of bacon and even more sausage. The guys shooed him out of the kitchen, insisting he was the groom, and as such, he should be getting ready for the wedding.

"It's not for another eight hours," he protested.

"So, you need to go relax and stay in the house,

out of target range," Collin said. "I spoke with Hank Patterson this morning. He said he'd be here before noon with a handful of his guys to sweep the area."

"Good. I'm not the only person who could be hurt if someone starts shooting. We should limit the number of guests to those who are willing to risk being in the line of fire."

"Good point," Percy said. He placed a hand on Gavin's back and turned him toward the living room. "Go shave, or something. And it wouldn't hurt to shower. You smell like horse shit."

Gavin glared at Percy. "Kiss my—"

"Gentlemen," Hannah cleared her throat. "We have a wedding to pull together in a short amount of time. I need all hands on deck. The chairs and tent will arrive in..." she glanced down at her watch, "ten minutes. I need you to help unload, set up and erect the items being delivered."

Percy, Collin, Franklin, Vasquez and Young headed for the door.

When Gavin started after them, Hannah stepped in front of him. "Not you. I need you to stay indoors until the event. We need you alive for the actual ceremony."

Gavin laughed. "And after?"

She shrugged. "It would be nice if you hung around for the honeymoon. Most brides prefer to have their grooms with them for that."

His head jerked up. "Honeymoon?"

"That's right," she said, her gaze locking on him. "Hank's treat."

He lowered his eyebrows. "Do I get a say in all of this?"

"Not really." Hannah smiled and patted his cheek. "Oh, quit belly-aching. You love her, and she loves you. You're getting a good deal out of this. Let's make the wedding memorable. You won't get a do-over."

"Love?" He looked at Hannah as if she'd lost her mind. "I just met the woman."

"And you're going through with a wedding." Hannah blinked. "The Gavin I know wouldn't marry anyone he didn't care about. He wouldn't say *I do,* unless he had feelings for the woman. What else could it be but love?" She grinned.

"Pity? Insanity? Brain damage, maybe. But love?" He shook his head. "Isn't that stretching a three-day relationship a little?"

"I knew I loved Taz in about the same amount of time. When you know, you just know." She clapped her hands. "Now, stop wasting my time. I have a million things to do." She turned and shouted, "Lori! Where are you? Time to get this show on the road."

"Coming!" Lori came limping into the kitchen.

"Go," Hannah said to Gavin. "You smell like a barn. Get a shower, use some cologne, iron your tuxedo. We want you to impress the princess. Dude, you're marrying up! Just be glad she doesn't want a pre-nup." She leaned close and hugged him quickly. "I'm so happy for you."

Gavin was ushered out of the kitchen and told to go up the stairs to his room.

"No peeking at the bride," Lori called out. "It's bad luck."

"Luck, schmuck," Gavin grumbled. He had a good mind to knock on Aurelia's door just to prove there was no such thing as luck.

He even raised his hand but thought better of it at the last second. He wanted to see her, if only to prove she was still there. What if she'd gotten cold feet and ran off before the wedding? Gavin leaned his forehead against the door and called out softly. "Aurelia, are you in there?"

For the longest moment of his life, there was no answer.

His heart stopped for that moment, and he held his breath.

Then she answered. "I am."

He let go of the breath he'd been holding in a whoosh. "Are you okay?"

"I'm fine," she answered, her voice soft, but close, as if she were standing on the other side of the door, as close as he was.

"Is that good fine? Or read between the lines, I'm-dying-here fine?"

"Good fine," she said.

"Okay, just checking." He should have moved away from the door, but he didn't. He wanted to be with her. To hold her in his arms and tell her everything would be all right. "We've got this, babe," he whispered. And then he pushed away from the door and went into his room to gather his things for a shower. He had a wedding to get ready for. And he wanted to look...and smell...his best. He was marrying a princess. He didn't want to scare her away before she made it to the altar. It was then that he realized he wasn't mad at her anymore. He was worried about her. She had a huge burden resting on her shoulders and someone trying to sabotage her commitment to taking care of her subjects. She'd done what she had to in order to ensure her country wouldn't fall into the wrong hands. Aurelia—no, Princess Olivia—would be a fair and just leader of her country, and Gavin would do whatever it took to help her in her efforts.

ON THE OTHER side of her door, Aurelia brushed an errant tear away from her cheek. This wedding was all wrong. Gavin was a good man who deserved a woman who had his best interests at heart. Not a woman who could only think of herself and her country. He had no idea what the pressure of being in the public eye at all times was like, or the amount of diplomacy needed to navigate the swamp of world leaders. He'd be miserable in Lastovia, away from his beloved Montana.

After seeing some of the beautiful state, Aurelia could understand the depth of his love for his home. She felt horrible asking him to leave it to join her in Lastovia. But she'd have to spend the majority of her days there. And any child that came along would have to be raised a royal to understand his or her place in society and among world leaders.

Oh, what she wouldn't give to have her brother and parents back. They could continue the St. George reign, and she could just be Olivia, a girl who liked to travel, a girl who wanted to marry a cowboy and live in Montana where they would raise half a dozen children who looked just like their father.

Another tear rolled down her cheek. Hell, she had to pull herself together. A bride couldn't show up to her wedding with red-rimmed, bloodshot eyes.

She could hear Gavin's door open and close, and then the door across the hallway open and close. He'd be taking a shower, getting ready for the wedding.

Aurelia gathered her toiletries, underwear and the white, fluffy bathrobe Hannah had brought to her earlier for her to use while she prepared for her wedding. When she heard Gavin leave the bathroom and return to his room, she crossed the hallway and stepped into the bathroom that was still steamy from

Gavin's use. She stood for a moment, inhaling the scent of his cologne, wishing he was there to hold her in his arms. He made her feel safe, even when they'd been standing naked in chilled water, with bullets flying all around them. She'd been certain he would protect her with his life, if it came down to that. He was that kind of man. Honest, kind and courageous. She couldn't ask for a better husband. But he could ask for a better wife, or at least one more suited to him and his way of life.

With her mind whirling through everything that had happened in the past week, she couldn't get a single thought to stick for more than a second. She pushed everything to the back of her mind, stepped beneath the shower's spray and closed her eyes. Immediately, she was transported back to the pool, standing in the rush of the cool, clear waterfall with Gavin. Her heart swelled, filling with all the emotion she couldn't suppress when she thought of the big, strong Navy SEAL. He was the kind of man a woman dreamed of.

After her shower, she rubbed sweet-smelling lotion into her skin, dried her hair and pulled it up into a loose messy bun, allowing tendrils to fall around her ears. A knock sounded on the bathroom door, making her jump and drop the brush she was holding in her hand.

"Aurelia?" Hannah's voice sounded through the paneling. "You need to start getting ready. Lori,

Sadie, Allie and I are here to help. You can come out. The coast is clear. Gavin's downstairs with the men."

Aurelia cinched the belt on the robe and stepped out of the bathroom.

"Oh, I love what you did with your hair," Hannah exclaimed. "And I'm glad you haven't done your makeup yet. Sadie brought her magic. She's going to help you with it."

The women ushered her into her bedroom and went to work getting her ready. Sadie applied the makeup while the rest of the ladies put on their bridesmaids' dresses. When Sadie finally stood back with a satisfied smile, she tried to turn toward the mirror.

Sadie shook her head. "Not yet. You want to get the full effect after you put on your dress."

While she'd been in the bathroom, someone had delivered the fully altered wedding dress and hung it on the back of her door.

Hannah and Lori pulled it off the hanger and held it while Aurelia stepped into the froth of lace, satin and tulle. Lori helped her place the veil in her hair and adjusted the train.

All the women stood back and gave a collective sigh.

"You're stunning," Sadie pronounced and then turned her to the full-length mirror.

Aurelia didn't recognize the woman staring back at her. She couldn't recall a time when she'd looked this beautiful. Suddenly, everything was all too real. Her heart leaped in her chest and pounded so hard she could hear her pulse beating against her eardrums. She needed to get outside, to breathe fresh air.

"Aurelia?" Hannah gripped her shoulders. "Are you okay?"

She shook her head. "I need air."

"You're having a panic attack, sweetie. Just breathe in and out."

When Aurelia tried to breathe in and out, she felt like her lungs weren't cooperating. Like she was trying to suck air through a wall.

"Do you want me to get you a paper bag to breathe into?" Hannah asked, her brow furrowed.

"No. I need air."

"What can we do?" Lori asked.

"Give her room," Hannah said.

"I need outside." Aurelia gathered up her dress and ran for the door.

Allie, Sadie's sister-in-law, was closest and opened it for her.

Aurelia darted out and raced down the steps and out the front door onto the deck.

Once outside, it still wasn't enough. She couldn't stop until she got to a place where the air wasn't so thick.

A whinny sounded from around the back of the house.

The barn.

Aurelia ran across the grass, rounded the corner of the house and headed straight for the barn. Once inside, she went straight for Sassy's stall. "Oh, Sassy. I don't…know…what…to do." She sucked in air, but it didn't seem to fill her lungs.

Grabbing hold of the latch, she pulled it open and slid the stall door to the side.

Sassy danced around the interior, tossing her head, excited, probably thinking she was going for a ride.

With everything seeming to crowd in around her, Aurelia could think only of escape. She had to get to a place she could actually breathe.

With the urgency of one starving for air, she flung a saddle over Sassy's back, cinched the girth and slipped a bridle over her head. Then she placed her satin clad food in the stirrup and swung up onto the horse's back.

At that moment, someone opened the big barn door. "Aurelia?" a voice called out.

Gavin.

Aurelia shook her head, her chest so tight she couldn't take even the tiniest of breaths. "I'm sorry," she said.

Spying sunshine and freedom, Sassy leaped forward, brushing past Gavin as she made a break from the confines of the barn.

Once outside, fences surrounded them.

Sassy didn't let that slow her down. She raced for the closest one and leaped over the top rail.

Aurelia held on, adjusting to the horse's movement. Soon, they were galloping across the pasture, heading away from the wedding and toward the safety and obscurity of the mountains.

CHAPTER 15

"Was that our bride?" Franklin ran across the barnyard toward Gavin.

"Damn it, yes!" Gavin ran toward Ranger's stall, ripped it open and led the horse out. In less than a minute, he had a saddle and bridle on him, but he knew Sassy and Aurelia were so far ahead of him that he'd struggle to catch up to her before something terrible happened.

Though Hank's men had arrived and had combed over the area within sniper range of the wedding tent, he couldn't be certain a gunman hadn't moved in after the Brotherhood Protectors had completed their scan.

Aurelia could be riding right into danger.

"You can't go after her," Percy called out. "You're in just as much danger, if not more, than her."

"I can't let her go. She could be hurt or killed."

Gavin stepped into the stirrup and flung his bum leg over Ranger's back. Percy tucked his prosthetic foot into the stirrup and jumped back.

Gavin raced for the pasture.

Vasquez already had the gate open when he reached it, allowing Gavin to gallop through.

Engines revved behind him. Hank's men would be mounting all available ATVs. When they ran out of ATVs, the rest would follow on horseback.

Gavin couldn't think about them, but he knew they'd have his back, if they got to him in time.

Why in hell had Aurelia run? Apparently, she'd had second thoughts.

His heart squeezed tightly in his chest. That she felt she had to run to keep from marrying him hurt more than he'd ever thought it could. As much as he wanted to marry Aurelia, he wouldn't if it made her miserable. She deserved to be happy. If it was with someone else, so be it. But right then, she was in danger. Gavin wouldn't stop protecting her just because she didn't want to marry him.

Ahead, he could see the billowing white wedding gown flying out behind the horse, racing across the pasture.

Sassy was fast, but Ranger was bigger, stronger and even faster, and he liked being first. Slowly, they were catching up to the other horse and the runaway bride. He had to catch them before Sassy tried to take another fence. She'd been running long enough, she had to be tired. If she attempted a jump, she might miss and catch her legs on barbed wire.

Gavin couldn't let that happen. He pressed his heels into Ranger's flanks, urging him to go even faster.

When he was abreast of the runaways, he reached across, grabbed the reins from Aurelia's hands and pulled back on Sassy's reins and Ranger's at the same time, digging his heels into his stirrups. "Whoa!" he shouted.

By the time he had both horses stopped, they were inches away from a barbed wire fence.

Sassy reared and danced, pulling at the reins, her eyes wide and wild.

Trying to keep his seat, hold Ranger's reins and keeping Sassy from dumping her rider, Gavin swore. Finally, he reached across, plucked Aurelia from the saddle and dragged her across his lap. When he released Sassy's reins, the mare bolted and ran back toward the barn.

Aurelia leaned into his chest, her breathing ragged, her eyes as wide and wild as those of the horse she'd been riding.

"Hey, shh," he said softly. "It's okay. I've got you now."

"It's not okay," she said, shaking her head. "I can't marry you."

"You don't have to do anything you don't want to

do," he said, though it hurt. He wanted her to marry him. "I just want you to be happy."

"You would be miserable if you married me," she said. "Life as a royal isn't all roses. It's work, and you're hounded by the paparazzi. There's never a moment that you're not worried someone will take what you say wrong. I can't do that to you."

"I know that. If it's so bad, why don't you let it go?"

She laughed, her voice catching. "I can't leave my people to my cousin. He's a terrible human being. But I'll have to since I'm not going to marry you. You would absolutely hate it. And we wouldn't be able to live in Montana for long."

"Wait." He pressed a finger to her lips. Hope swelled in his chest. "You won't marry me because you think *I'll* be miserable?"

She nodded. "I *know* you'd be miserable."

"Sweetheart, I've known misery. Being up to my elbows in sand and bullets in over one hundred and twenty degrees heat is misery. Running into cameramen and reporters is nothing in comparison."

"We'd have to live in Lastovia for most of the year. Montana is too far away for me to be an effective leader for my people."

"Who said I wouldn't go to Lastovia?"

"But you love it here," she said, looking into his eyes. "It's beautiful, and it's your home."

"Haven't you heard?" He touched the strand of

hair curling down around her ear. "Home is where the heart is," he said, his voice dipping lower. "The question is, where is your heart, Princess Olivia?"

She sucked in a breath, and her eyes filled with tears.

"Uh-uh." He held up his finger. "No tears, or you'll ruin your makeup. I have it from a reputable source the famous Sadie McClain did your makeup." He winked. "So, where is it, Aurelia. Where is your heart?"

She blinked away the tears and pressed a hand to his chest. "Right here," she whispered. "You are where my heart is. Wherever you are."

"And mine is with you." He leaned forward and pressed a kiss to her lips.

Gunfire ripped through the silence.

Gavin ducked his head while wrapping his body around Aurelia to shield her from lead poisoning.

Ranger stepped sideways and pranced, anxious to move.

"We need to go," he said. "Question is, do we make a run for it and forget everything, including Lastovia, or go back and have a hotdamn wedding?"

Another shot rang out.

"Wedding. Go back to the wedding," Aurelia blurted and clung to him.

Gavin pulled on the reins, turning them around. Then he sank his heels into Ranger's flanks.

The horse leaped forward, galloping as fast as he

could with two riders on his back.

The ATVs roared into view.

Gavin slowed long enough to point out the direction he thought the shots had come from. Then he continued toward the ranch house.

When he arrived in front of the house, the ladies hurried down from the porch and helped Aurelia down. Hannah carried a rifle.

Gavin didn't dismount. Instead, he reined around, back toward the action. "I'll be back in time to say I do. Don't start without me."

"No, Gavin. He'll kill you," Aurelia cried out.

"Not if I kill him first."

"Then you'll need this," Hannah said and handed him the rifle.

Gavin held the gun with one hand and the reins in the other, as he raced away, determined to put an end to the terror Aurelia had been living.

Ranger stretched out, eating away at the ground in long, fluid strides.

Gavin leaned over his neck, urging him to go even faster. When he got back to where he'd first heard the gunfire, he could see Hank's men combing through the underbrush, searching for the shooter.

Gavin dismounted from Ranger and studied his surroundings with the eye of a sniper. If he wanted to kill someone, the best location would be on higher ground, looking down. He scanned the area, looking up into the hills.

Hank's men had had the same idea and were working their way up the side of a steep ridge.

Something flashed in the sunshine above where Collin was climbing. Then an engine revved, and a man on a dirt bike took off, racing across the top of the ridge, heading back toward the ranch and the highway.

Being on top of the ridge, the man would have to come down soon. And coming down was much slower and more dangerous than going up.

Gavin mounted his horse and nudged Ranger into a gallop, paralleling the ridgeline. He knew the trail that led up to that ridge and where it would eventually come out. With that location in mind, he bent over the horse's neck and let him have his head. Ranger blasted across the valley.

When he reached where the trail would come down off the ridge, Gavin pulled hard on the reins and brought Ranger to a halt. Then he dropped to the ground, tucked Ranger behind a stand of trees and bushes and ran back to hide close to where the dirt bike would come out.

As he expected, the rider raced down the hill toward Gavin who hid in the shadows until the bike came abreast of his hiding place.

Gavin reached out, grabbed the guy's arm and yanked him off the bike. The motorcycle flipped onto its side and slid sideways the rest of the way down the hill.

The man who'd been riding it came up fighting.

Gavin wanted to bash the man's brains against the rocks, but he couldn't. He had to keep him alive to find out who had hired him. He would be the key witness in a case that would send a criminal to jail for murder and attempted murder. With that in mind, Gavin yanked the man's arm behind his back and pulled it up sharply between his shoulder blades. Then he ran him up against a tree, hitting his head hard enough to stun the guy, but not kill him.

Hank's men arrived in time to help him secure the man and carry him back to the ranch house where Hannah had had the foresight to have Sheriff Barron waiting to arrest him.

Once the authorities had cleared out, Gavin looked around for Aurelia.

"She's upstairs brushing the dust out of her hair and off her gown." Hannah smiled. "But don't worry, she'll be down."

"Are you sure?"

Hannah nodded. "I don't know what you said to her, but she's not afraid anymore. What was it she said? Oh, yeah. *Wild horses can't keep me away from marrying that man.*"

"Speaking of which…"

"Sassy is safely back in her stall and munching on grain." Lori pointed to the house. "Go wash up. The preacher's waiting."

"I don't care if Aurelia has dust in her hair. Tell

her to get down here. I don't want her to get a wild idea and run out on me again." He said his words loud enough the woman they were intended for could hear.

"I'll be down in just one minute," Aurelia called out from the upstairs landing.

"You better hurry," Hannah said. "A princess does not like to be kept waiting."

Gavin ran for the bathroom washed his hands and face and brushed the dust off his tux. In less than a minute, he was back out in the living area, waiting at the base of the staircase for his bride.

"You're supposed to wait with the preacher," Lori said.

"To hell with tradition. She's marrying me. She can walk down the aisle with me."

Aurelia appeared at the top of the staircase, carrying a bouquet of red roses. A strange young woman stood behind her, dressed in a long, pale pink dress, her face split in a happy grin.

Aurelia stared down at Gavin, a smile spreading across her face, lighting the room.

He held his breath as the most beautiful woman he could ever have imagined walked down the curving staircase to be with him.

"I'm the luckiest one-legged cowboy alive," he whispered into her ear and offered his arm. "Who's the lady behind you?"

"My best friend from Lastovia." She turned and

waved her hand toward the strawberry-blonde. "Lili, meet Gavin. Gavin…Lilianna."

"Nice to meet you, Gavin," Lilianna said, her cheeks turning a pretty pink.

Gavin took her hand. "The pleasure's mine."

Lilianna leaned close to Aurelia. "He's even more handsome than his profile picture."

Aurelia's gaze never left Gavin's. "Yes, he is."

Gavin's chest swelled so much he feared it would burst. This woman was about to promise herself to him.

She laid her hand on his sleeve and walked with him out of the house and across the lawn to an arbor that had been festooned with dozens of pink and white roses.

In a blur of words and nods, Gavin promised to love honor and cherish for the rest of his life this woman he'd known only three days. But he'd never been more certain of his decision as when he said *I do*.

When the preacher said he could kiss his bride, the Navy SEAL gathered her into his arms and gave her a kiss that would make her want to stay with him for the rest of her life.

When he let her up, her face was flushed and wreathed in a smile.

"Don't worry, princess, there's a lot more of those where that came from."

CHAPTER 16

Nine and a half months later...

Queen Olivia Aurelia St. George Blackstock stood on the balcony of the palace overlooking the largest crowd she could remember ever gathering to greet the royal family. Sadly, the royal family consisted only of herself, her husband, Gavin, and the baby girl growing in her belly. But she felt optimistic about her family's future and knew more children would come.

She rested her hand on her baby bump. As if on cue, Princess Hannah Lili Lori gave a healthy kick, reminding her that she was past due and ready to get out of the tight confines of her mother's belly.

"How are you doing?" Gavin asked, as he smiled toward the crowd.

"Much better now that the trial is over and my

cousin Rupert will spend the rest of his life in jail for the murder of my parents, brother and my two unfortunate fiancés." She sighed and pasted a smile on her face for the people who'd gathered to celebrate her coronation. With her birthday only a couple weeks away, and her baby due to arrive any minute, the parliament had convened and concurred that she had met her obligation and should be crowned before the baby came.

"Now that you've been here for a few months," Aurelia said, "any regrets?"

"Only one," he said and kissed her temple.

"Really?" she glanced up at him, her brow furrowing.

He rubbed his thumb across the lines on her forehead, smoothing away her frown. "I regret that I didn't meet you sooner. I've wasted so many years we could have been together."

She laughed and leaned into him. "We have many more ahead of us to make up for it."

"Yes, we do." He slipped his arm around her. "I'm glad the courts and solicitors were able to piece together everything Rupert did to your family. I can't believe he got away with it for so long."

"If you hadn't caught the shooter, he might have been the new king of Lastovia." She shuddered. "I hate to think of how he would have destroyed our country."

"I hate to think of how he might have hurt you." Gavin's arms tightened around her.

"But that's all behind us."

"Yes, it is. And now you're a queen."

"And you're about to be the proud papa of a princess." Aurelia tilted her head and looked up at her husband. "Do you miss Montana much?"

"What did I say?" he reminded her.

"Your home is where your heart is."

"Do you think Collin will find someone in Montana?" Aurelia asked. "I was surprised he chose to stay."

"Hank wanted him to head up a branch of the Brotherhood Protectors that would work out of Brighter Days Rehabilitation Ranch. He was happy to stay."

"Do you think he has a thing for your friend Lori?"

Gavin shrugged. "If he does, he'll have his hands full. She's a real ballbuster."

Aurelia laughed. "Then he's met his match." She rubbed her belly. "I probably should get off my feet. And my back is hurting a lot more than usual."

"Wave goodbye to your people. They love you almost as much as I do," Gavin said.

She raised her hand and started to wave, when a pain ripped through her belly and a gush of water slipped down her legs. "Oh, boy," she said and doubled over.

"Aurelia?" Gavin leaned over her. "What's wrong?"

"Nothing," she said, through her clenched teeth. "My water just broke."

"Seriously?" He straightened and waved at the crowd. "Show's over. Thanks for coming. Gotta go." Then he scooped her up in his arms and carried her back into the palace, shouting, "Call the doctor, boil some water, get the nurses, we're having a baby!"

Aurelia laughed and grunted as another pain tore through her. She didn't care, she was happier than any queen had a right to be. She had the man she loved caring for her and a baby girl ready to take the world by storm. She was the luckiest woman in the world, and she was even more in love now than she'd been on the day she'd married her Navy SEAL.

THE END

Thank you for reading Montana SEAL's Mail-Order Bride. The Brotherhood Protectors Series continues with SEAL Justice. Keep reading for the 1st Chapter.

INTERESTED IN MORE MILITARY romance stories? Subscribe to my newsletter and receive the Military Heroes Box Set

https://dl.bookfunnel.com/tug00n7mgd

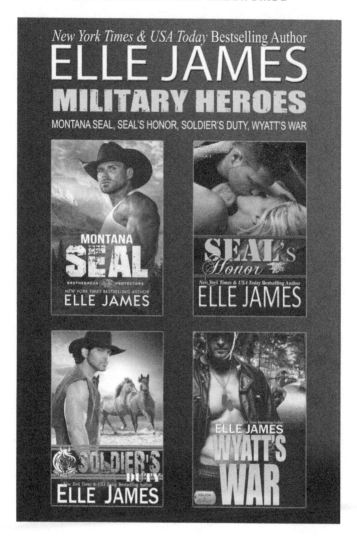

Visit ellejames.com for more titles and release dates
For hot cowboys, visit her alter ego Myla Jackson at
mylajackson.com
and join Elle James and Myla Jackson's Newsletter at
http://ellejames.com/ElleContact.htm

SEAL JUSTICE

BROTHERHOOD PROTECTORS BOOK #13

New York Times & USA Today
Bestselling Author

ELLE JAMES

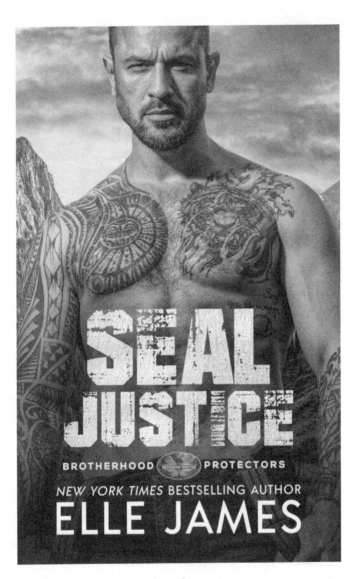

SEAL JUSTICE

BROTHERHOOD PROTECTORS

NEW YORK TIMES BESTSELLING AUTHOR

ELLE JAMES

CHAPTER 1

Reggie McDonald held her breath and listened for him. She shivered, her naked body chilled by the cool damp air of her prison. Though her brain was murky, her thoughts unclear, and her strength diminished, she knew what she had to do. When she could hear no sounds of boots on the wooden steps leading down into the earthen cellar, she continued digging. Inch by inch, she scraped away at the soil of her cell, praying she was correct in assuming hers was on the edge of the group of cells. If she dug long enough, she might see daylight and find a way to escape the hell she'd been trapped in for what felt like a lifetime.

Using the tin cup she'd been given to drink from, she scooped dirt from the corner behind the door. That small space was hidden from her captor when he came to feed her or shackle her to take her up to the big house where he tortured her and the other young women he'd kidnapped and held in the horrible dungeon beneath his house.

If she got out, she'd find help to get the other women out and save them from the sociopath who forced them to bow to his bidding. If they didn't do what he said, he whipped them with a riding crop or shocked them with a cattle prod. Sometimes, he burned them with the lit end of the cigars he smoked.

To keep them pliant to his will, he drugged their food and water, making them weak and groggy, unable to form clear thoughts or fight back.

Reggie had caught on to what he'd been doing. She couldn't quit eating or drinking completely, but she'd skip a day and use that time of semi-clear thinking to work through the problem to come up with a solution. On those clear days, she'd acted just as drugged when she'd been shackled and taken up the wooden stairs to the Master's house. When she could see out a window, she'd determined the house sat on the side of a hill, the slope dipping downward from the back of the structure. Though the women were trapped in the cellar, the earthen walls of their prison couldn't be that thick, especially on the far end where she was being kept. The hill sloped sharply on that end, giving her hope that, with steady digging, she'd eventually break free of captivity and escape.

Reggie prayed she was correct and scooped faster, pushing the soil she'd dislodged into the sides of the walls and floor, packing it down so that her captor couldn't tell it was fresh dirt.

She paused again as a sound penetrated the wooden door of her cell.

Footsteps.

"He's coming," a voice whispered. Reggie recognized Terri's voice. She was in the first cell, closest to the stairs. She'd been there the longest. A single mother of a little girl, she'd held out all those days, suffering through the torture in hope of seeing her little girl again. Lately, she'd fallen into despair of ever escaping.

Quiet sobs sounded from other cells along the row.

Reggie emptied her cup, quickly patted the dirt she'd removed into the ground, dragged her tattered blanket over her naked body and moved to the opposite corner where she curled up and pretended to be asleep.

Boots clunked down the steps to the bottom.

Silence reigned, even the few sobs ceased as the women held their breath, praying the Master wouldn't choose them for the trip up the stairs.

Reggie waited, listening. When a door hinge creaked, she braced herself.

"Please, no. Please," a woman's voice pleaded with the Master. It was Beth, a young college student who'd been captured on her way home from a night class. "Don't hurt me," she cried.

"Shut up and move," the Master's harsh voice echoed in the darkness.

"No, please. I can't." The sharp crackle of electricity sparking was followed by a scream.

Reggie winced and bit down hard on her tongue to keep from yelling at the man for hurting Beth. She couldn't draw attention to herself. Not now. Not when the hole she'd been digging was already two feet wide and as deep. If he took Beth up to the house, he'd be distracted long enough Reggie might finally break through.

Beth cried as she stumbled up the stairs, the Master's footsteps sounding as he climbed up behind her.

As soon as the door clicked closed at the top of the stairs, Reggie grabbed her cup and went back to work, digging furiously, scraping the dirt away with the cup and her fingernails. The Master usually kept a woman up in the big house for at least an hour before he brought her back to her cell. She didn't have much time.

She abandoned quiet for speed and dug as fast as she could.

"What are you doing?" Terri whispered, her voice barely carrying above the scraping sound of the cup on dirt and rocks.

Reggie ignored her, determined to get as far as she could before the Master returned.

Her cup struck a large rock. Undeterred, she

scraped around the edges, her heart beating faster, her breath coming in ragged gasps. The drugs in her body slowed her down, making her want to crawl into her blanket and sleep. But she couldn't.

"Stop whatever you're doing," Terri said.

Reggie halted and listened. When she didn't hear footsteps or the quiet sobs of Beth being returned to her cell, she went back to work on digging around the rock.

Soon, she found the edge of one end of the stone and worked her way around it.

After scraping and digging for what felt like an hour, she poked through the dirt and felt cool, fresh air streaming through a tiny hole onto her fingertips.

Not trusting her hands, she pushed her head through the tunnel and sniffed fresh air, the scent of decaying foliage a welcome scent from the earthen cell. She inhaled deeply, her breath catching on a sob. She'd been right. Her cell was on the edge of the hill. If she dug a little more, she might be able to push through. The large rock was in the way. If only...

She pulled her head out of the tunnel and shoved her bare feet in and pushed as hard as she could.

The rock didn't move.

Lying on her back, the cool dirt floor making her shiver, she scooted closer, bunched her legs and kicked hard with her heels, over and over until the rock moved. Hope blossomed in her chest and gave her the strength to keep pushing and kicking.

"You have to stop," Terri said. "When one of us crosses him, he punishes us all."

Another one of the women sobbed. "Please don't make him mad."

Reggie didn't want any of them to be hurt by her actions, but the Master was hurting them every time he took one of them up into the house. She had to get out and get help for all of them. Using every last bit of her strength to kick and shove at the boulder until it rocked and gave, she finally pushed it free of the soil, and it rolled down the hill. Loose dirt fell into the tunnel, blocking the sweet scent of fresh air.

Using her feet again, Reggie pushed at the dirt. More fell into the gap. She scrambled around and shoved her arms through the tight tunnel and patted the loose dirt against the walls of the tunnel, shoving the excess out and down the hill.

"Shh!" Someone said from one of the other cells. "He's coming."

A door opened above them. Sobs sounded as Beth descended into her prison, followed by the clumping sound of the Master's boots.

Reggie hadn't taken the time to pat the dirt into the walls this time. If the Master came into her cell, he'd catch her at digging her way out. She looked through the hole. Gray beckoned her. She shoved her shoulders through the tunnel. It was tight. Really tight. But if she could get her shoulders through, she could get the rest of her body through. Desperately inching and wiggling her way inside, she prayed she could breach the exit before the Master jerked open her door, grabbed her by the ankles and yanked her back inside. He'd beat her and chain her. And he'd throw her into the wooden box beneath the stairs where he kept the "naughty" girls.

No way. She couldn't let that happen. Not when she could taste freedom.

With her body blocking the tunnel, sounds of weeping and cries were muffled. Reggie couldn't tell if the women were informing the Master of her scratching and digging. She wasn't sticking around to find out. Once her shoulders were free, she braced her hands on the edges of the hole and pushed as hard as she could. Her body scraped through until her hips were free of the tunnel. Grabbing onto nearby branches, she pulled her legs out of the hole. Once all of her was free, gravity took hold, and she tumbled down the hill, her skin torn and gouged by sticks, rocks and bramble.

The jabs and tears made her cry out with joy. The pain wasn't inflicted by the Master but delivered by nature as a testament she was out of that hell.

She came to a stop when her head hit the big rock she'd pushed free of her tunnel. For a long moment, she lay still, her vision blurring, pain raking through the base of her skull.

Then she heard the sounds of dogs barking, and her heart froze. The Master had two vicious looking

Rottweilers he'd kept tethered when he'd brought her up into the big house.

Reggie staggered to her bare feet and shivered. The cool night air wrapped around her naked body. Swallowing the sobs rising up her throat, she ran, following the hill downward. She didn't know where she was or which way to go, only that she had to get as far away from the house and the dogs as possible. She hadn't come this far to be ripped apart by his maniacal dogs or dragged back to house and beaten until she couldn't remember who she was or why she cared.

Sticks and rocks dug into the soft pads of her feet, drawing blood. She kept running until her feet were as numb as her skin and mind. The dogs were getting closer. She had to do something to lose them.

The hill continued downward. A cloud crossed over the sky, blocking what little starlight penetrated the tree branches. Her lungs burning and her heart beating so fast she thought it might explode out of her chest, Reggie was forced to stop long enough for the cloud to shift, allowing the starlight to illuminate her way.

When it did, she stared out at a dark canyon. She stood on the edge of a precipice. Easing to the edge, she could see the glint of starlight off what appeared to be a river forty feet below where she stood.

The barking dogs were close now.

Reggie turned right then left. No matter which

way she went, the cliffs were still as high as the one in front of her. She couldn't backtrack. The dogs were so close enough, they'd find her.

She refused to give up. But what else could she do? Die from the vicious rendering of sharp Rottweiler teeth, go back willingly to the Master's house to be beaten, or jump off a cliff into water of which she had no idea of the depth?

When the barking sounded right behind her, Reggie spun to face the two Rottweilers, emerging from the tree line...stalking her.

A shout from behind them made her heart leap into her throat. The Master.

Without further thought or mental debate, Reggie turned and threw herself over the cliff.

As she plunged downward, she steeled herself for the impact against rocks or whatever lay beneath the water's surface.

Crossing her arms over her chest, pointed her toes and hit the river feet-first, sinking deep. The chill shocked her body, but she kept her mouth shut tight, and struggled, kicking hard to rise. Just when she thought she would never breathe again, she bobbed to the surface and gasped. Above her, she heard the wild barking of the Rottweilers.

The cold water helped clear her foggy brain. She had to make the Master think she was dead. Taking a deep breath, she lay over, face-first in the water and floated as far as she could before turning her head to the side to take another breath. She did this for as long as she could hear the dogs barking above. The Master had to think she'd died in the fall from the cliff. It was the only way to get away and make him think she couldn't tell the authorities about what he had hidden in his basement.

After a while, the sound of the dogs barking faded. Knowing the dogs couldn't follow her scent in the water, she let the river's current carry her along as she treaded water to keep her head above the surface.

The cold sapped what little energy she had left. She rolled onto her back and floated into the shallows where she dragged herself up onto the shore.

Darkness surrounded her, embraced her and sucked her under. As she faded into unconsciousness, her last thought was...*I'm free*.

ABOUT THE AUTHOR

ELLE JAMES also writing as MYLA JACKSON is a *New York Times* and *USA Today* Bestselling author of books including cowboys, intrigues and paranormal adventures that keep her readers on the edges of their seats. When she's not at her computer, she's traveling, snow skiing, boating, or riding her ATV, dreaming up new stories. Learn more about Elle James at www.ellejames.com

Website | Facebook | Twitter | GoodReads | Newsletter | BookBub | Amazon

Or visit her alter ego Myla Jackson at mylajackson.com
Website | Facebook | Twitter | Newsletter

Follow Me!
www.ellejames.com
ellejamesauthor@gmail.com

ALSO BY ELLE JAMES

Lucas (#3)

Beau (#4)

Rafael (#5)

Valentin (#6)

Landry (#7)

Simon (#8)

Maurice (#9)

Jacques (#10)

Brotherhood Protectors Yellowstone

Saving Kyla (#1)

Saving Chelsea (#2)

Saving Amanda (#3)

Saving Liliana (#4)

Saving Breely (#5)

Saving Savvie (#6)

Saving Jenna (#7)

Saving Peyton (#8)

Saving Londyn (#9)

Brotherhood Protectors Colorado

SEAL Salvation (#1)

Rocky Mountain Rescue (#2)

Ranger Redemption (#3)

Tactical Takeover (#4)

Breaking Rules (#2)

Breaking Away (#3)

Breaking Free (#4)

Breaking Hearts (#5)

Breaking Ties (#6)

Breaking Point (#7)

Breaking Dawn (#8)

Breaking Promises (#9)

Hearts & Heroes Series

Wyatt's War (#1)

Mack's Witness (#2)

Ronin's Return (#3)

Sam's Surrender (#4)

Hellfire Series

Hellfire, Texas (#1)

Justice Burning (#2)

Smoldering Desire (#3)

Hellfire in High Heels (#4)

Playing With Fire (#5)

Up in Flames (#6)

Total Meltdown (#7)

Take No Prisoners Series

The Billionaire Replacement Date (#8) coming soon

The Billionaire Wedding Date (#9) coming soon

Cajun Magic Mystery Series

Voodoo on the Bayou (#1)

Voodoo for Two (#2)

Deja Voodoo (#3)

Cajun Magic Mysteries Books 1-3

The Outriders

Homicide at Whiskey Gulch (#1)

Hideout at Whiskey Gulch (#2)

Held Hostage at Whiskey Gulch (#3)

Setup at Whiskey Gulch (#4)

Missing Witness at Whiskey Gulch (#5)

Cowboy Justice at Whiskey Gulch (#6)

Boys Behaving Badly Anthologies

Rogues (#1)

Blue Collar (#2)

Pirates (#3)

Stranded (#4)

First Responder (#5)

Silver Soldier's (#6)

Warrior's Conquest

Enslaved by the Viking Short Story

Conquests

Smokin' Hot Firemen

Protecting the Colton Bride

Protecting the Colton Bride & Colton's Cowboy Code

Heir to Murder

Secret Service Rescue

High Octane Heroes

Haunted

Engaged with the Boss

Cowboy Brigade

An Unexpected Clue

Under Suspicion, With Child

Texas-Size Secrets

Made in the USA
Monee, IL
06 August 2024

63377888R00138